KU-568-992

EMILY STEAD

ULTIMATE
FOOTBALL HEROES

LIONESSES
EUROPEAN CHAMPIONS

THE ROAD TO GLORY

DINO

First published by Dino Books in 2022,
an imprint of Bonnier Books UK,
4th Floor, Victoria House, Bloomsbury Square, London WC1B 4DA
Owned by Bonnier Books,
Sveavägen 56, Stockholm, Sweden

🐦 @UFHbooks
🐦 @footieheroesbks
www.heroesfootball.com
www.bonnierbooks.co.uk

Text © Studio Press 2022

Design by www.envydesign.co.uk

All rights reserved. No part of this publication may be reproduced, stored in a
retrieval system, or transmitted in any form or by any means, without the prior
permission in writing of the publisher, nor be otherwise circulated in any form
of binding or cover other than that in which it is published and without a similar
condition including this condition being imposed on the subsequent purchaser.

Paperback ISBN: 978 1 78946 688 1
E-book ISBN: 978 1 78946 695 9

British Library cataloguing-in-publication data:
A catalogue record for this book is available from the British Library.

Printed and bound in Great Britain by Clays Ltd, Elcograf S.p.A.

3 5 7 9 10 8 6 4

All names and trademarks are the property of their respective owners,
which are in no way associated with Dino Books. Use of these
names does not imply any cooperation or endorsement.

To fans of the women's game,
old or new,
everybody's welcome.

ULTIMATE
FOOTBALL HEROES

Emily Stead has loved writing for children ever since she
was a child herself! Working as a children's writer and editor,
she has created books about some of football's biggest stars,
teams and tournaments for many a season. She remains a
passionate supporter of women's football and Leeds United.

Cover illustration by Dan Leydon.
To learn more about Dan visit danleydon.com
To purchase his artwork visit etsy.com/shop/footynews
Or just follow him on Twitter @danleydon

TABLE OF CONTENTS

ACKNOWLEDGEMENTS

My first thank you is to Bonnier Books UK for adding me to their squad! Next thanks go to the dream team that is Matt and Tom Oldfield, guys who had the vision to create *Ultimate Football Heroes*, a series of books that continues to thrill young readers and football fans in their millions.

To every teacher, bookseller and librarian who has helped get the books into the hands of readers, special thanks are due. And of course, an extra-special mention goes to you, the readers and fans – without you there wouldn't be any Heroes.

I was hugely honoured to be asked to share the stories of England's Lionesses – European Champions, no less! – some of the best role models any footballer starting out in the game could hope to have. Theirs are stories of girls with incredible talent and winning mentalities, who dreamed big enough to achieve the greatest of prizes.

Before them though, a host of fearless women paved the way for women's football to grow into the game it has become today. Players like Lily Parr and Bella Reay who sadly never had the opportunity to play for an official England team, despite their lionhearted love of the game. Or Sylvia Gore and Sheila Parker who played in the first England match to be recognised by the Football Association, as late as 1972.

And to all the women who have since juggled studies, jobs and families, while entertaining crowds for little reward or, at times, none at all.

The fifty-year ban that so unfairly affected generations of women and girls has meant that the game is still playing catch-up to where it should rightfully be. But with our current squad of Lionesses who are fighting to give *all* young people the same opportunities to enjoy the beautiful game, women's football is in the best hands. Lionesses, your legacy as champions is set to go far beyond your achievements on the pitch. Thank you.

Finally, a massive thank you to my family, who lost me completely to football for a summer and kept the coffee flowing.

A.L.A.W.

EURO HEROES: THE DAY IT CAME HOME

31 July 2022, Wembley Stadium, London
Women's Euro 2022 Final – England vs Germany

Sweet Caroline,
Da-da-da,
Good times never seemed so good,
So good, so good, so good!

The final whistle blew. They had done it. England had won the Women's Euros for the first time in their history. On home soil. Against Germany, of all the teams! Sarina Wiegman had known this squad had talent when she took on the job as the team's new coach just months earlier, but even she hadn't realised just how special this group of players would prove to be. They had scored some unbelievable goals and put in performances to inspire a whole nation, in front of record crowds. Was the Lionesses' victory always written in the stars?

Chloe Kelly, scorer of the winning goal, raised her arms to the skies. Best friends Millie Bright and Rachel Daly hugged tightly, tears of joy rolling down their cheeks. Meanwhile captain Leah Williamson went straight to console the gifted young German, Lena Oberdorf, whose own tears would not stop flowing.

What had just happened? What had they done? No one could quite believe it. But it had happened. England were about to be crowned European Champions! These were the moments they had dreamed of their whole lives, and they were going to soak in every single second. Twenty-three Lionesses and their manager had become history-makers, and the party was not going to stop for days to come.

What's more, England had won in style. Anyone who argued that they weren't worthy champions would look pretty silly. England had entertained, dug in, and fought hard to beat the very best teams in Europe, winning armies of new fans up and down the country. Young or old, no matter your gender, or even what club you supported, everyone was welcome to share the Lionesses' special journey. They had thrilled crowds in the stadiums and caused TV audiences to leap from their sofas along the way. England had been:

Free-scoring in an 8–0 thrashing of Norway.

Unstoppable against the Swedes in the semi.

And determined to defeat Germany in an epic final.

The mighty Lionesses had roared to victory, showing skill and grit in equal measure, along with a team spirit that never once wavered throughout the whole tournament. Every single player in Sarina's squad had played their part to bring football home at last.

Squeezing the stories of all twenty-three Lionesses and their manager into just one book wouldn't do these girls justice. So this book shares the stories of four of them:

Lucy Bronze – a swashbuckling right-back who

conquered world football,

Ellen White – Lionesses legend and all-time record goalscorer,

Beth Mead – England's girl with the goal-den touch,

And **Leah Williamson** – wise beyond her years and rightly trusted with the captain's armband.

If you're ready to join each player on their journey, from pulling on her very first pair of boots to having a gold medal placed around her neck as a European Champion, then turn the page. These are players who dared to dream big, and whose dreams came true.

KICKING OFF

CHAPTER 1

ELLEN WHITE
A GAME OF TWO HALVES

It was a grey school day at William Harding Primary School. Ellen White's Year One class were sat cross-legged on the carpet, while their teacher held up some colourful flashcards.

'10 x 5... Who can tell me the answer?' she asked the class. 'Ellen?'

But Ellen wasn't listening. She was watching big, fat raindrops slide slowly down the window and staring out at the large grassy field beyond. That field was Ellen's very favourite place to be. The place where she a kicked a ball around with the boys every single playtime. Her shoes were scuffed and each day she'd come home with leaves in her hair from fetching the ball from where it often ended up... in the bushes. Luckily, her parents didn't seem to mind. They were as football crazy as she was!

'Ellen?' said the teacher again.

But just as Ellen was about to reply, the *DIINNNGG!* heralded morning playtime.

'Saved by the bell!' said Ellen under her breath, before rushing out through the cloakroom and onto the field.

The baby of the family, Ellen couldn't honestly remember a time before football. Her first memories were of taking on her big brother Marcus and sister in some epic battles in the garden. She may have been smaller than them, but she chased after the ball as though she were playing in a World Cup final. Dad Jon was always in goal, shouting advice, like: 'Take him on!' or 'Shooooot!'

As was common growing up in the 1990s, there wasn't a local girls' league, so Jon set up his own football academy. The Mini Ducks welcomed boys and girls. Although the sessions were all about having fun, it was clear to see that Ellen was a talented kid.

When she was eight, she joined her first junior club, Aylesbury Town, a boys' side. She counted down to the weekends, when she got to play proper matches. Just like at school, she was the only girl on the side. But not once did it cross Ellen's mind that she was somehow different from the boys. They treated her just like any other player, she was one of the team.

That same year, scouts came from London club Arsenal to watch one of the team's matches. Ellen did her best to impress them with her skills, and her eye for goal, and she was accepted to train at the club after school, two nights a week.

'Our very own Ells-Bells, a proper footballer,' her dad used to say on the long car journeys to north London. 'Next stop, Wembley Stadium!'

'No pressure, Dad!' Ellen would laugh.

Then one Sunday, minutes before Aylesbury's latest match was about to kick off, a man they'd not seen before appeared on the sidelines. He wasn't wearing a tracksuit, and he didn't look like the scouts Ellen had seen before. When the man approached the team's coach and asked for a 'quiet word', Ellen's dad Jon knew there was about to be trouble.

Ellen looked over at the three men from where she was warming up. She couldn't hear what they were saying, but could tell from their faces that something wasn't right.

A couple of minutes later, the man swiftly disappeared. Her coach walked over to Ellen and looked her straight in the eye.

'I'm so sorry, Ellen,' he said. 'That man was from the League.' He paused. 'They say you can't share a changing room with the boys. They won't let you play anymore.'

Nine-year-old Ellen's heart sank. She tried to speak, but only the tiniest breath would come out.

'Ridiculous!' Jon broke the silence. 'She's on Arsenal's books for goodness' sake and they won't let her play for some lousy Chiltern Youth League.'

'If it were up to me...' the coach's voice trailed off apologetically.

'Come on, Ellen,' her dad said. He snatched up her things and marched off towards the car park, his daughter trotting meekly by his side.

Back at home in her bedroom, Ellen asked to be left alone. There was nothing her mum or dad could say to fix things. Thoughts raced through her head.

How could this be happening? She'd played against boys her whole life! And scored over a hundred goals for Aylesbury last season. What about her teammates? Her friends?

Ellen buried her face in her pillow and screamed.

She wasn't sure how long she'd lain there, but when she opened her eyes again her face was red and blotchy. Ellen looked up at the tatty poster that had been stuck to her bedroom wall for years now, and her brother's wall before that. Gary Lineker, one of England's best-ever goalscorers, wearing the famous shirt of the Three Lions, stared back at her.

'This never happened to you,' she said sulkily.

*

23 September 1998, Aylesbury

The following Wednesday, Ellen's dad arrived home

early from work. He burst through the door, waving a copy of the local newspaper *The Bucks Herald* in the air.

'We've only gone and made the front page!' he cried, unfolding the paper, as his family gathered round excitedly.

'SOCCER GIRL BANNED BY LEAGUE FOR BOYS,' Ellen's mum read the headline aloud.

'Ellen is only nine and can't fathom why she can't play football...' Marcus read over his mum's shoulder. 'Great picture too!' he laughed.

Ellen stared at the glum-looking girl in the photo, dressed in her favourite Arsenal strip. And for the first time since Sunday, the smile returned to Ellen's face. She may have played her last match for Aylesbury Town, but she suddenly felt an enormous rush of love for her parents. She was glad they had spoken to the newspapers; there were bound to be other little girls just like her who weren't allowed to play the game they loved, when they too had done nothing wrong.

Ellen knew she was one of the lucky ones. She could still play football twice a week for Arsenal.

And the mighty Gunners were one of the best clubs in the whole country. She wasn't about to give up on her game any time soon.

CHAPTER 2

ELLEN WHITE
UPS AND DOWNS

Fast forward seven seasons, and Ellen's game had
gone from strength to strength. The tall sixteen-year-
old was on the fringes of Arsenal's first team, but
a place in the starting line-up still seemed a distant
dream. Arsenal Ladies, as they were known, were a
fearsome side, winning every trophy going. If Ellen
wanted to be the best she could be, she had to be
higher up in a manager's plans. So when the chance to
move to Chelsea came up, Ellen pushed her nerves to
one side and grabbed it with both hands. In her head,
she knew it was the right decision. Chelsea were a
club on the up, with ambitious plans to bring in more
top players.

*

'Three seasons in a row as top scorer!' Jon White said proudly at dinner one evening.

Things couldn't have gone much better since joining Chelsea. Ellen was stronger and fitter than she had ever been, and her touch in front of goal was becoming razor sharp.

The Blues had some top players in the squad. England international defender Casey Stoney and goalkeeper Siobhan Chamberlain led by example.

'You should see how hard they work in training, Dad,' said Ellen, munching on some broccoli. 'It's incredible! And that's after working all day in their real jobs.'

While Ellen was no stranger to hard work herself, having such strong role models around pushed Ellen to get even better. If she was going to reach the top, she had to keep up with the competition. Another young Chelsea forward, Eni Aluko, was only a couple of years older than Ellen, and she was already in the England squad!

'Keep going, Ellen,' Casey Stoney told her. 'Keep scoring those goals and your time will come.'

By now, Ellen had already been rewarded with call-ups to play for England's Under-17 and Under-19 teams. It was such an honour to be selected and pull on an England shirt. She felt a bit giddy when she stopped to think about it. Her best performance as a young Lioness had come when she'd hit a hat-trick in an Under-19s match against Poland earlier that year. They'd finished the match as 7–0 winners.

'It looks like you enjoyed that one, Ellen!' coach Mo Marley smiled.

Mo was right. Scoring goals and helping her team to win made Ellen feel incredible. But the teenager had an even bigger goal in her sights. She wanted to make the Lionesses' senior Number 9 shirt her own some day.

In the summer of 2008, Ellen was on the move again. This time, she was joining the talented team at Leeds Carnegie, an exciting new club that matched her own ambitions. They had made three cup finals during Ellen's time as a Chelsea player, but hadn't had the firepower to secure a trophy. Could Ellen prove the missing ingredient, so player and club could win their first trophy together?

But within months of signing for her new club, disaster struck for Ellen. She picked up a serious knee injury that would keep her out of the game for a lengthy spell. It had struck at the worst possible moment, when Ellen had been flying for Leeds.

What if someone else comes into the team and takes my shirt? Ellen was worried. It wasn't worth thinking about.

The journey back to full fitness was long and lonely. Not being able to kick a ball felt horrible, and she missed her teammates and being out on the grass more than she could have imagined. Plenty of playing careers had been ended by the infamous anterior cruciate knee ligament injury, usually when players tried to come back before they were ready, making the injury worse. Ellen had to be patient and keep working hard.

'One day at a time,' she reminded herself in the gym each session, while dutifully completing each boring exercise that the club's physio had prescribed.

Meanwhile, she decided to throw herself into her studies, glad of the distraction. On her sports science course at Loughborough University, Ellen studied alongside some of the best athletes in the country from all different sports.

P.E. had been her best subject at school and she hoped to find a job in sport one day. She knew that football alone wasn't likely to pay the bills.

As she sat in the university library one day, Ellen thought back to her schooldays. She remembered the time when her teachers were trying to spur her on to get a personal best in athletics, offering her chocolate biscuits if she beat her best time.

'Find me some strawberries and we have a deal!' Ellen remembered telling them.

That was just like Ellen. She understood the small things that all added up to make her the best she could be. Hard work. Healthy diet. Sleep. And practice, practice, practice. At that moment, it struck her just how much she loved football.

'I'll beat this injury, no matter how long it takes,'

she told herself.

Then after twelve painful months, the pain in Ellen's knee finally eased. Ellen returned to the pitch and the goals soon followed.

CHAPTER 3

LUCY BRONZE TOUGHENING UP

Born Lucia Roberta Tough Bronze, Lucy was not always the superstar who could deliver a pumped-up team talk in front of 87,000 fans, or crack a joke with a camera crew in her face. Growing up, she was a shy child who *never* shouted out the answers in class (even though she knew them all, especially the maths ones). But with a ball at her feet, Lucy was a different girl. On a football pitch was where she could shine her brightest. Here she formed friendships. Here she belonged.

Her mum Diane, a teacher, met Lucy's dad Joaquin in Portugal. Neither parent watched football on TV, or even understood any of the rules. Nevertheless, the couple would go on to raise three football-crazy children. Lucy was the middle child, with an older brother and a younger sister. Jorge was born in Portugal, but the family moved to Diane's home county of Northumberland before the girls arrived. Lucy's first years were spent on tiny Holy Island before a move to the suburbs.

When she was six years old, Lucy joined her big brother's team, Alnwick Town. Being the only girl didn't matter. There was no special treatment. Jorge didn't hold back in his tackles, and he never let her score.

'My ball!' said Lucy.

'No way!' argued Jorge. 'That was never a foul!'

The pair would squabble from morning until night if a football was involved, with neither parent keen to referee. What Lucy didn't realise was that Jorge's take-no-prisoners attitude was exactly what she needed to become a better player. The very best version of herself. If she wanted the ball, she would have to earn it.

The opposition teams underestimated Lucy. When they saw little Lucy line up alongside the boys, the players sniggered. And the parents were less kind still.

'Girls playing football? It's not normal,' they complained.

Girls shouldn't be strong, they shouldn't be competitive, was the message Lucy heard time and again. But she shrugged off the comments as easily as she shrugged off the tackles; her mum and dad hadn't named her 'Tough' by accident! No one was going to put Lucy off her game.

There were times when Diane wished her daughter wasn't quite so obsessed with football though, especially in those moments when Lucy would be practising her keepie-uppies in the kitchen while she was trying to make a cup of tea!

Diane encouraged Lucy's gift for tennis, but gave up when Lucy refused to wear the white frilly socks she'd bought for a tournament. Instead Lucy turned up in her full Alnwick kit and still won. The plain truth was this: football was what Lucy loved.

*

Then when she was eleven, her coach had to deliver

some heartbreaking news. Lucy couldn't play for her beloved Alnwick after the summer holidays. A Football Association rule meant that girls were banned from mixed teams after the age of twelve. It wasn't allowed. *It was 2002!*

The rule was supposedly brought in to protect girls from getting hurt, yet there stood Lucy, taller and stronger than most of the boys! When Diane had been born, women and girls were still forbidden from playing team football at all in England, a ban that lasted for fifty years. Sadly, the damage was still affecting women and girls generations later.

'Right,' huffed Diane, more to the universe than the poor coach. 'No one is telling my little girl that she can't do something!'

So Diane found Lucy an all-girls' side, Blyth Town, while she thought about how to tackle the unfair FA rule.

Unsure at first, Lucy began to enjoy mucking about with her new friends at Blyth and was scoring for fun. But it didn't match up to the rough and tumble of playing with the boys. She needed to be challenged, to play against the best.

The next step on Lucy's journey came when her team faced Sunderland, who arrived in Blyth one matchday wearing striking red-and-white-striped shirts and black shorts.

'They look like they're going on *Match of the Day*!' gasped Lucy, stretching her own hand-me-down shirt down to her thighs.

As the teams warmed up, everyone was buzzing about two of the Sunderland girls.

'See her,' said Blyth's goalkeeper. She nodded at a grinning girl, whose Afro hair was scraped back into a bun. 'She plays for England!'

'And her!' said another teammate, pointing out a slight, ponytailed girl, easily the smallest player on the pitch.

Wow! thought Lucy. She had no idea there even was an England team for girls! So, Lucy being Lucy decided that she wanted to play for England too. Her dreams of appearing at the famous Wembley Stadium some day began when she was aged twelve.

Both England girls impressed during the match.

The small one had enviable close control, and not one Blyth player could get past the other girl. The final score wasn't one for the scrapbook.

'You've got to get me in that team,' Lucy pleaded with her mum after the match.

'Are you sure, love?' Diane replied. 'It's quite a trip and you know what you're like on long journeys.'

But Lucy's mind was made up, and a trial at Sunderland was quickly arranged. Diane drove her daughter an hour-and-a-half south to the academy, with Lucy feeling carsick the whole journey. Thankfully, the trip paid off. The Teesside club nicknamed the 'Lasses' saw that Lucy had something special, and signed her up to their academy straight away.

Then began the long trips from Alnwick to Sunderland for training three times a week. Dinner was eaten in the car and homework written on the hoof, but the hard work soon paid off. Before the year ended, Lucy had been picked to join the England youth team too. The huge smile on her face said it all!

Oh, and those two girls' names, in case you were wondering... Demi Stokes and Jordan Nobbs.

CHAPTER 4

LUCY BRONZE
AMERICAN DREAM

Friday nights were family film night in the Bronze
household. This week was Lucy's turn to choose, so
she was thrilled when *Bend It Like Beckham* was still
on the shelf at the local video rental shop. The 2002
film follows the football journeys of two girls whose
skills (spoiler alert!) see them earn soccer scholarships
to the United States.

It may have been just a movie, but it sparked a fire
in Diane Bronze who began researching 'American
soccer schools' on the internet the very next day.
When she discovered an exclusive camp for girls,
Lucy begged her mum to sign her up, and North
Carolina became an unlikely holiday destination for

the Bronzes' family holiday that summer.

Women's football, or 'soccer' as it was advertised, was really taking off in America. When it came to facilities and coaches, England lagged far behind. The US women's team had twice won the World Cup, and top British players such as Kelly Smith and Julie Fleeting had crossed the pond to try to make a living from the game.

The camp was an experience that opened Lucy's eyes to what she could achieve. Playing alongside hundreds of girls, who loved the game as much she did and were just as good, quickly made her feel at home. In America, not only was it acceptable to be competitive and want to be the best, but it was actively encouraged.

'I'm not different here, Mum!' smiled Lucy.

Lucy's driving runs and hunger to win the ball caught the eye of one of the coaches.

'Bring her back when she's seventeen and I'll give her a scholarship,' Anson Dorrance promised.

So that's what happened. Lucy signed off at Sunderland with a player-of-the-match performance in her first FA Women's Cup final before heading to the University of North Carolina. Her team would be the Tar Heels, the best university side in America, while she studied sport too.

Lucy arrived to find that football and soccer were worlds apart. Stateside, even the university teams were sponsored, so all the latest football boots, trainers and kits came for free. In England not even the FA Cup had a sponsor! Lucy thought back to when she'd got her first pair of boots from the Argos catalogue. Nike Total 90s. She'd had to seriously sweet-talk her mum for those!

Trophies and honours were rewards for Lucy's strong performances in the Tar Heels midfield. Lucy was living her American dream! But just four months later, she received a letter with the official England letterhead. The letter came out of the blue with some unwelcome news.

'"We regret to inform you that while you are living in the United States, you will remain unavailable for selection to the England Under-19 squad",' Lucy read the letter out loud. 'What? This can't be happening!'

She wished her mum and dad had been there, but instead, 6,000 kilometres lay between them. They had never felt further away.

Lucy had an almost impossible choice to make: give up playing for the team she loved most in the world or end her American adventure early and come home. Reluctantly she returned to England and Sunderland. The decision felt right in her heart, and Lucy was glad to be back at home with her family, but thoughts still niggled in her head.

How good could I have been if I'd stayed? Lucy wondered.

*

Then during one England camp, when Lucy was eighteen, everything changed. She picked up a knock on her knee in training.

'It's not too bad,' she told the coaches at the time. But a few days later her knee became infected and she found she couldn't even run.

Doctors fitted a leg brace and Lucy was left

hobbling around on crutches. She couldn't drive, and sitting on the sidelines made it hard to keep up friendships. The only friends she had were footballers. The timing was terrible; she had been in such fantastic form.

Months later her knee still wasn't better. She felt miserable and alone. Neither her latest club Everton nor England had the funds to send their players to see a private doctor. Feeling desperate for her daughter, Diane paid the doctor's bills. Lucy had surgery and could finally start her road to recovery.

'We'll soon have you back to your best,' Diane promised.

That's the thing I love most about you, Mum, Lucy thought to herself. *You're always by my side.* But Lucy knew that if she was going to get back on her feet, she'd have to use every drop of her mental strength to get there. And it had to come from within.

So Lucy trained through the pain, pushing herself to the limit. All the time, not knowing it was the wrong thing to do. As a result, Lucy damaged her other knee. She couldn't play on. At last she saw a new doctor.

'You've been playing with torn cartilage,' the doctor told Lucy. 'I'm afraid you'll need a new operation to fix the problem.'

Another setback.

Then came the phone call from England's Under-23 coach. 'You should have looked after yourself better, Lucy,' he scolded the young player. 'We won't be picking you for the squad again.'

The words hit Lucy like a steam train. She'd been injured on England duty, she'd received no medical help, and now she was being told it was all her fault!

Without football, she was lost.

'You can do this, Lucy,' Diane kept reminding her. This time she chose her words carefully. Getting back to her 'best' would take an almighty effort, and even then it wasn't guaranteed.

There were days when Lucy felt like giving up football for good. If people asked, she began introducing herself as a student, rather than a footballer. But she loved football, so she kept going.

Although no one could say when she would be able to get back on the pitch or even kick a ball again, Lucy completed every single mind-numbing exercise that would get her back to full fitness.

To Lucy's surprise, it wasn't her physical injury that had hurt the most. What felt worse was seeing the friends she had grown up with, like Jordan Nobbs and Toni Duggan, pushing ahead without her. While they were experiencing the thrills of playing in European Championships with England's young Lionesses, Lucy was relegated to the sofa. All because of a freak injury. She was happy for them, of course, but desperately wished that they were all flying off together.

Then, finally, the day arrived when Lucy reached her end goal. Her knees had healed and she was back in the game.

CHAPTER 5

BETH MEAD
JUMPERS FOR GOALPOSTS

'Dad!' called Beth. 'Can you help me with my laces?'

Seven-year-old Beth Mead sat on the step outside her front door, clutching a battered leather football, itching to get out to the park with her friends.

In the tiny fishing village of Hinderwell at the edge of the North Yorkshire moors, there wasn't much for the kids growing up there to do if they didn't like football. There were two pubs and a hairdresser's. The nearest shop was about a mile away. It was the sort of place where sheep easily outnumber people.

The local park had one set of metal goalposts and no net, with the players' abandoned jumpers making up the second goal. It was perfect for playing games of

Three-and-In or *Wembley Cuppies* every day until it got too dark to tell the teams apart.

Beth had had her first taste of football aged six, when she joined a Saturday morning football session in that same field. It was her mum's latest plan to help her daughter burn off some energy.

The coach had welcomed Beth, the first girl that had come to train.

'The boys can be pretty rough,' he warned.

But one hour later, Beth had proved she was at least as rough as anyone on the pitch.

'She's quite a talent, your daughter,' the coach had said to Mrs Mead. 'You should try to find her a club where she can play with other girls.'

He wasn't trying to exclude Beth – quite the opposite. A pathway in girls' football could lead her to great things. But for the next few weeks, the park was Beth's home ground.

Opposite the park was Beth's gran's house, where Beth would dash for a glass of water or quick toilet break between matches. It was also the place where Gran served up Sunday lunch for the family. It was

Beth's favourite meal of the week: roast beef, loads of veg and cauliflower cheese, with Gran's glorious Yorkshire puds saved to eat last!

Beth was in the middle of helping clear the plates one afternoon, when right on cue, there was a knock at the door. Three boys in tracksuits, almost threadbare at the knees, stood there sheepishly.

'It's for you, Beth,' her gran called. 'The only visitors I get are ones who want you to play football!' she said with a wink.

Beth leaned in to plant a kiss on her grandmother's cheek as she bustled past her. 'Thanks for dinner, Gran!' she smiled.

Beth and the boys headed to some nearby garages where a goalpost had been painted on one of the garage doors. Each time the ball hit it, making a heck of a racket, everyone scrambled to volley or head the rebound.

One day her mum announced that she'd found Beth a girls' club. California Girls FC were located half an hour from Hinderwell.

'Not too bad!' smiled Mum, as she filled in the

registration form.

When she looked up at her daughter, though, the colour had completely drained from Beth's usually rosy cheeks.

She'd never played with girls before.

What if they don't like me? What if I'm not good enough? The thoughts raced through Beth's mind. Her stomach felt as though it were twisting into knots.

The following week, and with much coaxing, Beth agreed to go with her dad – just once – to see what it was all about.

'Give it a chance,' said Dad, as they pulled into the car park.

'I'm sorry Dad, I just can't,' cried Beth, in floods of tears.

Beth's dad had learned to deal with his daughter's anxiety. Usually, he could talk her round, but try as he might, this time he couldn't persuade her to even get out of the car. Suddenly he smiled.

'Look, love!' he said. He nodded his head towards the next pitch where the boys' teams were playing.

Seconds later, and as if by magic, the car door

clicked open. And so it was decided. Back with the boys on the California Boys team was where Beth would play next!

*

Beth's first cup tie with the California Boys was away to a club in the suburbs of Middlesbrough. She often got nervous before a big match, but today she was feeling more anxious than ever.

'What's that little girl doing playing for you?' sneered one boy, who could easily have passed for a secondary school pupil. He was at least a foot taller than Beth.

'Couldn't you find eleven boys?' one of his teammates laughed.

Beth felt both cheeks flush pink, and her heart began to race. 'I can't do this, Dad,' she cried.

But Richard Mead smiled kindly, and gave the same reply as always. 'Don't forget,' he began, putting his hands on her shoulders. 'The bigger they are, the harder they fall.'

And just like that, Beth's nerves melted away.

After that she played like a Yorkshire Terrier. The first to every ball, she never let her head drop. Then came her chance to get one over on one of the boys, when a fifty-fifty ball fizzed their way. Beth crunched into the tackle winning the ball and sent the boy flying. He landed in a crumpled heap as a sudden silence passed through the crowd.

'Tackled by a girl, eh?' said Beth, jumping back to her feet. *He wasn't laughing now!*

After that, Beth decided that if she could brave the tackles of the biggest boys, she was ready to give girls' football a go.

CHAPTER 6

BETH MEAD
ADDING TO THE ARSENAL

A short stint at California Girls came next for Beth, before scouts from Middlesbrough spotted her talents. Beth's face had lit up when she found out that Middlesbrough wanted her.

'We think you have what it takes to do well here,' Andy Cook, a coach at the Centre of Excellence, told the ten-year-old.

Training would be twice a week, and Beth's mum June had to take on an extra job to cover the cost of the petrol they would need to get to the academy, a forty-five-minute drive away.

Middlesbrough was the largest town on Teesside, yet not massive by national standards. Compared to Beth's tiny village, though, it may as well have been London. In just a few months, it was where Beth would also attend secondary school, and go from knowing every single face to recognising hardly anyone. The thought filled her with dread.

The academy, all sparkly and new, had impressed Beth and the coaches seemed to know their stuff. But now on their second trip to Middlesbrough, the fear factor was well and truly kicking in. Beth was desperate to play, but sometimes got herself so worked up about whether she deserved to be there. She wanted to tell her mum to turn the car around. Then she could go back to playing on the village field with the boys and the odd roaming sheep. She was always happy there.

'I don't think I can do this,' she said, trying to force back the tears.

'It will all be worth it, love!' Beth's mum promised, looking back at her daughter through the rear-view mirror. 'Wait and see.'

June was right, of course.

'I scored four goals!' Beth proudly told her mum

after training.

'My player of the match!' June smiled.

*

Six happy years at Middlesbrough FC and Beth's
stay at the club was about to come to an end. The
option to stay until she turned seventeen was there,
but when Sunderland showed interest in the young
striker, Beth couldn't turn them down. She was ready
to break out of her comfort zone and the Lasses played
in the FA Women's Super League 2, the second-
highest division in the country!

Not once did Beth regret her decision. In her very
first campaign, Beth finished as top scorer, helping her
side to win promotion. It was the first of three busy
seasons at Sunderland. Beth balanced her university
studies and working in a pub with banging in the
goals. She loved every moment.

Her Sunderland stats were so good (seventy-seven
goals in seventy-eight appearances) that Arsenal tried
for two years to bring her to London, before she

eventually agreed to join the Champions League club. Signing for the Gunners meant that Beth could train full time. No more pulling pints at the weekend – and she'd finished her studies too.

'Now I can relax and concentrate on my football!' she told friends and family, thrilled.

In her short career, everything Beth touched had turned to gold. The goals had been flowing and she'd won a whole load of trophies. But on the road to stardom there are always bumps, as Beth was about to find out.

In her first few months at Arsenal, Beth made the Number 9 shirt her own. She hadn't stopped scoring since Sunderland, and she'd loved getting to know the fans at Meadow Park. Signing autographs and taking selfies was part of her job now.

Then ahead of the new season, Arsenal announced another signing that would change everything. Two years younger than Beth, Vivianne Miedema – Viv for short – was one of the hottest young strikers in the world. Every top club from Europe to the United States had been vying for her signature, but

Viv had chosen England and more precisely Arsenal. Unsurprisingly, the Dutch striker went straight into the team.

To find herself sat on the bench felt to Beth like a kick in the teeth, a feeling she hadn't felt before. Beth had started almost every game since she was a kid!

Beth gave her all in training, shooting from all angles, but it was like she was trying too hard to impress. One day when she was chasing after a ball she was never going to reach, she slipped and injured herself. With a broken collarbone, she was set to be sidelined for weeks.

While her body began to heal, Beth's confidence was shot. Dad will know the right words to say, she thought.

'What am I supposed to do?' she asked him on the phone. 'I've moved my whole life to London and it's all falling apart.'

'You've got two choices, Bethy,' Richard said calmly. 'Come home with your tail between your legs, or stay and fight for your place. We both know you're good enough.'

His words may have sounded harsh, but Richard knew his daughter well. The advice was exactly what Beth needed to hear. Then after six long and frustrating weeks, Beth was ready to join her teammates again. As she ran out onto the training pitch, it felt so good to feel the grass underneath her boots.

'I've missed this!' She smiled to her teammates.

But before Beth had even kicked a ball, the coach Pedro Martínez Losa called her over. Little did she know that this was about to be one of the most important conversations of her life.

'Hear me out,' Pedro began. 'I want to try you as a winger.'

'Me on the wing, really?' Beth replied, rolling her eyes dramatically.

Pedro nodded, and began to talk more about the role he wanted her to play.

That night in bed, as Beth tossed and turned, she thought back to the conversation with her coach and let her thoughts play out.

I've been a Number 9 since I was a little girl. What if I'm rubbish as a winger? She worried too about missing the buzz of the ball hitting the back of the net. *Goals are what my game's about!*

Then she thought of the positives. She knew what strikers liked, early crosses to run onto and shoot. If she could figure out how to put in those balls, being out on the wing could actually work. Besides, Pedro was a fantastic manager. *He knows what he's doing, right?*

So Beth worked hard to adapt her game and win her place back in the side. Sure, she hated her new position at first, but before long Beth was getting regular minutes on the pitch again, with Arsenal and England's Under-23s.

CHAPTER 7

LEAH WILLIAMSON
ODD ONE IN

'Can Grandma take me today?' Leah asked her mum, one Saturday morning.

It was time for training at Scot Youth FC, the club that Leah Williamson had joined a few months earlier. As the only girl in a boys' team, Leah may have been the odd one out, but the boys had become fiercely protective of the latest addition to their squad. Why wouldn't they look out for her? After all, with Leah on the side, they stood a much better chance of winning.

'If she's good enough, she'll play,' the coach had promised Leah's mum before Leah's very first session.

And play she did. What a talent!

Six years old and it was obvious even then.

Whether it was splashing about at the swimming pool or tumbling at gymnastics, Leah was a natural at any sport she tried. Oddly, it was her gym coach who had first introduced Leah to football, throwing a ball into the gym at the end of one class for the girls to chase after. From that moment, for Leah, having a ball at her feet felt like the most natural thing in the world.

So Amanda Williamson had had to put aside her own painful experience of playing football as a child, stories she didn't share with Leah until years later, and let her daughter try football for herself. Amanda had wanted to play so badly that she'd had to cut her hair and pretend to be a boy to escape the nasty comments from opposition teams and their parents.

Leah's club was based in Bletchley, Milton Keynes, where the railway line ran right alongside the pitch. When the trains rattled past in the middle of a match, it was impossible to hear a thing. But that didn't matter to Leah. That bobbly pitch was her Wembley.

'I'll give Grandma a call now,' Leah's mum replied. 'But you're going to need this.'

She picked up a small plastic case from where it had

been discarded on the floor. Inside was a gumshield with an England flag on it. Amanda had bought it out of fear, because the teams they played tried to kick lumps out of her daughter.

It's only natural that Mum worries about me. I get that, thought Leah. *But none of the boys have to wear a gumshield!*

And what Leah's mum didn't know was that Grandma Bernie didn't make her granddaughter wear one either!

Grandma Bernie and Amanda were two of Arsenal's most loyal supporters, while Leah's dad David and younger brother Jacob followed Tottenham Hotspur. It made for some interesting TV viewing when the family came together, especially when the two north London clubs went head to head in the Premier League. Leah had decided that like the females in her family, she too was a Gooner, and wore the Number 14 shirt of her hero, Arsenal's Thierry Henry, with pride.

It was the very same shirt that Leah was wearing when her grandma arrived to collect her that morning. As usual, Grandma Bernie stayed to watch training.

In the space of a few short months, Bernie could see for herself just how much her granddaughter had improved. Leah was so calm on the ball, making graceful runs and completing thoughtful passes that put her team one step ahead of the opposition.

'Great cross, Leah,' Bernie called, clapping her hands. She watched as her granddaughter high-fived a tall boy in a yellow bib who had latched on to Leah's pass to score.

As well as being a skilful player – she had soon learned to run rings round the boys – Leah was a caring kid. The first to check on a teammate if they'd been fouled, the player that rallied the team if they went a goal behind, Leah was a leader even at such a young age.

'Future Arsenal captain?' suggested a dad on the sidelines, as Leah organised the team huddle.

'You never know!' Bernie chuckled.

*

The next rung on the ladder for Leah was a try-out

at Rushden and Diamonds' Centre of Excellence for a girls-only team. The fancy-sounding academy gave the best girls in the area the chance to play together. Located almost thirty miles from home, its proper pitches and positive coaches made the long trips worthwhile.

'It's worth it just to see that great big smile of yours,' Leah's dad smiled, putting an arm around his daughter at the end of her latest training session.

'My coaches say I'm doing pretty well, Dad,' Leah beamed. 'I've just got to keep working hard.'

Hard work had never been a problem. Leah trained harder than any of the young footballers at the academy and hung off every last instruction the coaches gave her. These past few years at Rushden and Diamonds had seen her improve as a player every season.

'Still think you'd look good in a Spurs shirt!' Dad teased.

'No way,' Leah bristled. 'Gooners for life!'

CHAPTER 8

LEAH WILLIAMSON
ALL ABOUT ARSENAL

A couple of weeks later, Leah received some unexpected news. One of the Diamonds' coaches announced she was leaving to go to work at another club. As she was the first female coach that Leah had had, the pair had formed a strong bond.

'Do you have to go?' asked Leah, tears pricking the corners of her eyes.

'Let me get settled,' her coach promised. 'And we'll get you along to Arsenal for a trial.'

'Your new club is... Arsenal?' Leah cried in disbelief.

She couldn't believe her luck. Arsenal! The club where Thierry Henry plays! Kelly Smith! *The club I've supported my whole life!* An incredible opportunity could be heading her way.

Leah felt nervous and excited as they arrived for her trial at Arsenal's London Colney training ground. She knew it was her one chance to impress, a chance she'd have to grab with both hands. Leah was crazy about Arsenal and the thought of being an actual player for the same club as her heroes sent shivers down her spine.

'How do you think you did?' the coach asked later on.

'Yeah, not bad,' Leah replied.

Then he smiled. 'We'd like you to join us here at Arsenal if that's OK?'

She had passed her trial with flying colours!

OK? OK? This is the best thing that's happened in my whole life! thought Leah.

'Say yes then!' smiled Amanda, hugging her daughter.

'YESSS!!!' smiled Leah. 'Gooners for life!'

*

By now, Spurs supporter David Williamson had accepted the fact, rather begrudgingly, that his daughter was Arsenal through and through.

'Come on you Reds!' he'd cheer when he came to watch Leah in action. But he couldn't quite bring himself to say the name of his bitter rivals! Still, their family holiday to Cornwall would give them all a break from football. Or so he thought...

In the middle of a game of beach cricket, Amanda's phone rang. It was someone from the club, asking whether Leah would like to be a mascot for the men's team.

'There's just one problem,' said Amanda. 'The match is away to West Brom, that's hundreds of miles away!'

'Please can I do it? Please?' nine-year-old Leah begged her parents.

Looking into Leah's pleading eyes, Amanda realised they didn't have much choice! She knew how much it would mean to her daughter.

'Start packing your things then,' Amanda said, with a smile.

'Yesss!' Leah smiled back, pulling her shirt over her

head as though she'd just scored a Cup Final winner.

The next morning Leah and her mum set off on the long drive to the Hawthorns. They joined the rest of the family back in Cornwall the day after the match. Leah had loved every minute of being a mascot and was bursting to tell her dad and brother all about it.

'I even had a photo with Theo!' she beamed.

Theo Walcott was the club's new teenage winger who had been part of England's World Cup squad aged just seventeen!

Things at Arsenal were going well, and Leah was in the perfect place to learn her trade. The women's first team were unstoppable, winning trophy after trophy. Sometimes the players would drop by when the girls were training, offering tips and encouragement. Stars such as Kelly Smith, Rachel Yankey and a young Alex Scott were some of the finest talents in the women's game. Leah couldn't have wished for better role models.

When Leah was ten, she was a mascot again, this time for England, as the Lionesses tried to qualify for the 2011 World Cup. Amanda took a photo of Leah standing proudly next to her Arsenal and England hero Kelly Smith, which the forward later signed.

To Leah,
Dream big!!!
Best wishes,
Kelly Smith 10

The photo took pride of place stuck to the mirror of Leah's dressing table. Leah looked at it every day, but knew that 'Dreaming big' would only take her so far... it was hard work on the pitch that counted. Like Kelly, Leah was a fighter, prepared to do whatever it took to make her dream of reaching the top come true.

Just as important were Leah's studies off the pitch. That had been drilled into her from a young age. Her mum and dad explained that out of even the biggest stars, legends of the women's game, only a handful of players managed to earn a living from football. So, homework was always handed in on time, reading books were finished, and projects were completed as best as they could be. A Maths whizz, Leah's head for figures came in handy when studying football statistics too!

*

Then in 2012, Leah was chosen to train with the Lionesses Under-15s.

When her mum had read the email, she'd almost burst. 'My daughter, an England star!'

Testing herself against some of the best young players in the country was set to be Leah's biggest challenge yet. It would also mean that Leah would be away from home for three whole days and nights, not knowing a soul.

'Be yourself and they'll love you.' Amanda hugged her daughter goodbye. 'Guaranteed.'

Leah smiled. She knew how lucky she was to have a family who believed in her, but they were biased of course.

On day one of camp, Leah was keen to be the first one down to training. First impressions counted. She had been at Arsenal for six years now, where everything was so familiar. Her teammates, the staff, the training ground. Here she was on her own, the only girl from Arsenal to be called up.

But when she got down to the pitches, a few of the girls were already warming up. Closest to her, a trio dressed in the sleek black England training kits they had all been given were passing the ball in little triangles.

Leah set her eyes on one girl with strawberry-blonde hair who was about the same height as her. She was pulling off perfect little flicks and turns, laughing and joking with each touch. Leah was mesmerised. *How can she be so calm?* It seemed to Leah like she'd played for England for years!

Next to the girl, Leah cut a shy and awkward figure, homesickness already starting to creep over her.

If I'm going to get through this camp, I have to make that girl my friend! Leah resolved, feeling like the geekiest teenager in the world. *Just as long as she doesn't find out about my Star Wars bedcovers. Definitely not cool.* Leah quickly pushed the thought out of her mind.

'You joining in?' said the girl, noticing Leah standing by herself.

'Sure,' said Leah, hoping she wouldn't notice her

suddenly crimson cheeks.

The girl's name was Keira Walsh, she played for
Blackburn Rovers Academy and spoke with a strong
northern accent. Like Leah, she was football crazy
and had supported her local team, Manchester City,
since she was tiny too it turned out.

From that moment on, Leah and Keira became
inseparable, and by the time they turned seventeen,
within days of each other, they were two of the
most promising young players in the country. Leah's
maturity and caring attitude had led her to be named
captain, a responsibility which helped her game thrive
even more. Meanwhile Keira read the game so well.

Captain or not, having Keira by Leah's side – when
times were tough and the team was far from home –
made the journey so much easier.

YOUNG LIONESSES

The more matches these four gifted girls played, the more they understood why it was called the beautiful game. On a football pitch was where some of the best moments of their lives had taken place.

Ellen White bounced back from injury and moved around a few top clubs in search of silverware. Her willingness to work hard, and of course her goals, made her a first pick at every club she signed for.

Lucy Bronze juggled her studies and job in a pizza parlour alongside her first senior football contract on her return from a stint in the USA.

Beth Mead left her home in north-east England, swapping Sunderland for the big city and Arsenal. She also switched roles too, giving up her Number 9 shirt to discover her true talents as a winger.

Leah Williamson became Arsenal's homegrown hero, cementing her place in the side after making her first-team debut aged just seventeen.

The four had all proudly played for England's youth teams, but winning a first cap for the senior team of Lionesses would be the greatest honour of their lives. Growing up, Ellen White and Lucy Bronze hadn't even known there was an England Women's national team, the aftershocks of a fifty-year ban on women's football. A few years later, as the game kept growing, a young Beth Mead and Leah Williamson were lucky enough to have some top women's footballers as role models.

Now it was time for Ellen, Lucy, Beth and Leah to raise their game to the next level.

CHAPTER 9

ELLEN WHITE
DREAM DEBUT

It was March 2010 when Ellen got the call she'd been dreaming of since she was a kid. The one where the manager of England says she wants you to join her squad. Ellen was so excited, she'd nearly dropped her phone!

The young forward would be joining the Lionesses for their important World Cup qualifier against Austria, a strong side themselves. Better still, the match was going to be played in west London, not far from Aylesbury, the town where Ellen had grown up.

She called home straight away, bursting to share the good news with her family.

'You going to come and watch then?' Ellen asked

jokingly.

'Try and stop us!' her dad replied.

The night of the match quickly came around. Ellen stared at the team sheet taped to the dressing room wall. Listed among the substitutes, there was her name in black and white: Number 17, ELLEN WHITE.

Picked to start up front were Lianne Sanderson and Eni Aluko, but Kelly Smith – who played her football in America – had had to be scrubbed from the line-up at the last minute with an injury. England weren't about to risk their record goalscorer with a World Cup ahead of them.

'How are you feeling, Ellen?' a woman with long plaited hair asked her. It was Jill Scott, another young player with a bright future ahead of her.

'Good,' Ellen replied. She was so nervous, it seemed her brain would only let her give one-word answers.

For Ellen, it was such an amazing feeling to be sharing a bench alongside the likes of Kelly Smith and Jill Scott. These were players who already knew what it felt like to play in a World Cup, the most important and exciting tournament in women's football. What

Ellen would give to experience that for herself!

The match kicked off and an early goal gave England the lead. At half-time, neither team had added to the score, but it was England who looked the more dangerous. After the break, Ellen headed to the subs' bench with Kelly filing in after her. She sat down on one of the blue plastic seats behind Ellen.

'You know you might get on tonight?' Kelly leaned into Ellen's ear.

Ellen nodded back and smiled, not really believing the words of her new England teammate. From the outside, Ellen may have looked calm, but what Kelly didn't see was that both Ellen's legs had begun to shake like jelly.

Focus on the game, Ellen said to herself.

With half an hour to go, England were 2–0 up and heading for a comfortable win. The game looked done and dusted, and they weren't under any pressure to score again. Just then, the assistant coach came over.

'Start warming up, Ellen,' he called. 'You're coming on.'

After a quick run and some stretches, Ellen stripped

down to her playing kit. Red shirt. White shorts.
White socks. Classic.

The ref's assistant held up the electronic board.
Number 17 replacing Number 2.

This is really happening! thought Ellen.

She stood there for what felt like hours, pulling
up her socks and fiddling with her hair, until finally
it was time to go on.

The head coach Hope Powell stood close, and gave
Ellen a little pat on the back as she ran onto the pitch.
'Go score me a goal. Enjoy it,' she said.

'Got it, boss!' Ellen nodded.

Ellen had never felt so nervous or excited in her
whole life. She was full of respect for the manager,
but the ex-England hero cut an intimidating figure at
times. If Hope Powell told you to score, then that's
what you did.

Ellen took up her position on the left wing.
With each touch of the ball, her confidence grew,
as electricity began to flow through her body. Just
do what you do, she reminded herself.

You'd never have known the ground was less

than a quarter full from the noise the crowd was making, Loftus Road was buzzing! And before long, so was Ellen.

With the seconds ticking down in the final minute of the game, Ellen knew it was now or never. She collected a pass out wide and surged past a tired Austrian defender. The angle was tight, but Ellen still had the goal in sight. As the keeper came rushing out towards her, Ellen dinked it cleverly over her with her weaker left foot. Time seemed to stand still as two defenders slid desperately towards the ball, but neither could stop it from crossing the line.

GOOOAAAAALLL! She'd done it! It was such a special moment. Ellen hadn't for one second dreamt she'd score on her debut, and in the final minute too!

'What a fantastic goal to mark her first game for England,' the commentator told the TV audience watching at home. 'It's a beauty!'

High-fives and hugs from her teammates followed. The next moments were a blur, and then, at last, the final whistle blew. 3–0. Full time. What a debut!

'Ellen White will remember this moment for as

long as she plays football...' The commentator paused dramatically for his final sign-off. 'And well beyond.'

As Ellen walked off the pitch, her whole body tingling, she spotted her family waving wildly in the crowd. She grinned and waved back, making a heart sign with her hands. There was no better feeling in the world.

'Welcome to the Lionesses!' Her old Chelsea teammate Casey Stoney smiled.

CHAPTER 10

LUCY BRONZE
AGAINST ALL ODDS

Lucy's next move came in 2012, when Liverpool
swooped for the young defender. Only days earlier,
England star Fara Williams had become a Red too.
A Lioness, no less! Now was Lucy's chance to learn
as much as she could from Fara and the other top
players around her.

As Fara ran riot in midfield, Lucy claimed her place
as a regular starter in Liverpool's defence. The team
moved up through the gears and in 2013 wrestled the
Women's Super League title away from Arsenal.

Lucy was playing better than she ever had, but her
efforts – it seemed – were going unnoticed by her
country. She wondered what else she had to do to

get in the England senior team.

'Why won't they pick me?' Lucy asked her mum and dad, fed up.

A few years earlier, before all Lucy's injuries, a coach from the Portugal national team had got in touch with Diane Bronze when it was revealed that Lucy was half-Portuguese. Facebook could sometimes be useful!

'If Lucy ever decides to play for Portugal,' the coach had messaged. 'Your daughter would be very welcome.'

'Maybe I should swap sides and play for your country, Dad?' Lucy wondered out loud one day.

'It's your decision,' Joaquin told his daughter. 'We can't make it for you, but whatever you decide, we'll stand by you.'

Then, just as Lucy was about to give up on England, she got the call. The senior squad had some players out with injury and were drafting Lucy into the side for the upcoming friendly against Japan. She had waited so long to be selected and that shirt meant so much. Lucy couldn't wait to be a Lioness.

*

26 June 2013, Pirelli Stadium, Burton upon Trent

Pulling her socks up high over her knees, Lucy could hardly contain her excitement. She allowed herself a quick glimpse around the dressing room. Alex Scott. Casey Stoney. Rachel Yankey too, the first player in the women's game whose shirt Lucy remembered asking for. All England legends!

Play well and I might even make the Euros squad! was the thought buzzing through Lucy's mind.

The following month, England would fly out to Sweden for the 2013 Women's European Championship and take on the best nations in Europe. But Lucy knew she couldn't look too far ahead. First, she had to impress against Japan. And the *Nadeshiko* would be no pushovers – they were world champions!

England started the game well and grabbed a first-half lead thanks to Eni Aluko. They kept pushing for a second goal, but couldn't find a way to score. Then it was time. Hope Powell looked sternly over her glasses at Lucy. 'You're on,' she said.

A sixty-seventh-minute sub, Lucy was determined to make every minute of her time on the pitch count. No one was about to get past Lucy Bronze! Hope Powell was furious soon after though, when a sloppy Fara Williams pass allowed Japan to equalise.

Then with seconds to go Lucy found herself in the box. As the ball was flicked on, Lucy scrambled the ball home for a last-minute winner. But to everyone's confusion, the assistant on the far side of the pitch raised her flag. Offside!

It would have been nice to grab a debut goal and the winner for her team, but since childhood Lucy had always taken far more pleasure from stopping goals than scoring them. Never one for the limelight, she just hoped she'd done enough to win a second cap.

And she had.

'You looked comfortable out there,' Hope Powell told her. 'If you can do that against the World Cup winners, maybe you can do a job for us?'

Lucy grinned.

The fact that the Lionesses were hit by a number

of injuries worked to Lucy's advantage: she was good enough to play anywhere along the backline and even in midfield. So the following month, Lucy thanked her lucky stars when she found herself in the squad for the 2013 Euros. Exciting times lay ahead!

But the 2013 tournament came and went without Lucy playing a single minute. Defeats to Spain, France and a draw with Russia saw England exit the competition with a whimper. Hope Powell, England's pioneering manager, who had taken charge of the team for fifteen years, was sacked soon after. Would whoever came in next pick Lucy? There were no guarantees.

CHAPTER 11

BETH MEAD
A LIONESS'S PRIDE

'Am I on speakerphone?' Beth bellowed down the phone line. 'Mum, Dad, I'm a Lioness!'

It was April 2018, and after her strong performances as a winger at Arsenal, Beth had earned her first call-up to the England senior team. With two World Cup qualifiers to play, this was Beth's chance to show what she could do.

'Fantastic!' said her dad, Richard. 'We couldn't be prouder!'

Two substitute appearances and four points later, Beth had loved the whole experience of playing for England, and her new teammates had made her feel so welcome. The feedback had been good – the coach wanted to add more young players to the squad, and twenty-two-year-old Beth was one of them.

'If you keep playing like that,' Phil Neville said, 'a first start won't be far away.'

Beth was over the moon! When she stopped to look back on things at the end of the season, she could see just how far she had come on her footballing journey.

Then in September it happened. Beth's full debut. Having clinched their place at France 2019 just days earlier, the Lionesses were on a high. The coach made good his promise and gave seven players their full international debuts. Beth was among them, wearing the Number 11 shirt for the away match in Kazakhstan.

It took her just nine minutes to make an impression, scoring from the penalty spot shortly after being chopped down in the box.

'Great pen, Beth!' the coaches on the bench applauded.

Midway through the second half, Beth had the chance to double her score, but saw her penalty bounce back off the post.

'Unlucky,' said captain Keira Walsh. 'Let's go again.'

And that's just what Beth did. Undeterred, she rolled home her second goal, and England's fifth, late in the match. Final score 6–0.

Back in the dressing room, Beth was buzzing. It felt brilliant to play all ninety minutes. She took off her red shirt and touched the badge with the famous Three Lions.

'I'm framing this one!' she told her Arsenal teammate, Leah Williamson.

'You could have had the match ball too, if that post hadn't been in the way!' Leah joked.

*

27 February 2019, SheBelieves Cup, USA

When the plane had touched down on the runway at Philadelphia Airport a few days earlier, the temperature had been freezing. Now on the day of England's opening match in the SheBelieves Cup, it wasn't any warmer.

'This should suit us better than it suits Brazil!' Beth joked to Lucy Bronze, as the pair worked on their pre-match stretches.

'We've got this,' said Lucy confidently.

Both players had grown up in the north-east of England where cold and drizzle came with the territory. They weren't about to let bad weather affect their game.

But Brazil posed a massive threat. With legends like Marta and Formiga, they were deadly in attack. In the first half, England looked sluggish. Sloppy passes, leggy runs, the Lionesses were way off the pace. Was jet lag to blame?

Whatever the reason, they had to address it quickly. They were 1–0 down to a soft penalty at half-time, and someone needed to step up and score.

Fran Kirby was a player who could be relied on to take a game by the scruff of its neck and that's exactly what happened late on. Ellen White had already levelled the scores, and England were pushing to grab the winner. Fran picked up a Keira Walsh pass and drove into space. As two Brazilian defenders approached, Fran nudged the ball to Beth out wide on the right wing.

Beth had been on the pitch less than ten minutes, but saw the chance open up in front of her.

I have to hit this, she thought instinctively. She put her laces through the ball and rifled it into the top corner, beyond the reach of the keeper. *Gooooaaaalllll!*

'Stunning!' said the TV commentator. 'Absolutely stunning from Arsenal's Beth Mead!'

Back in Yorkshire, Beth's parents were watching bleary eyed. But when they saw their daughter's shot sail in, they forgot all about the five-hour time difference!

'Did you mean to shoot?' gasped Ellen, the first to reach Beth before the rest of the team mobbed the winger.

'Sure did!' Beth beamed.

And she had. It hadn't been a fluke. A carbon-copy goal for the Under-20s in Canada and many more sensational strikes for Arsenal were proof of that. Beth had laid down a marker to be included in the World Cup squad that summer, and she'd done all she could. Now it was up to the gaffer.

CHAPTER 12

LEAH WILLIAMSON AS SURE AS FATE

The date 7 June 2018 would forever be etched in Leah's memory as the day she made her England debut. The twenty-year-old had been called up as part of the Lionesses squad to face Bosnia-Herzegovina and Kazakhstan the previous winter, but she hadn't got on the pitch. Still, just being named in the same squad as the likes of Fara Williams and Steph Houghton was a humbling experience. There was so much that Leah could learn from watching players like these. How they behaved on and off the pitch, how they treated teammates and staff, even what they ate.

England thrashed both teams in the end, while Leah watched from the bench.

This camp in Russia, though, felt different. Leah had been in fantastic form for her club and was now a fan favourite and first-team regular at Arsenal. Meanwhile England had appointed a new manager, who was keen to refresh his squad with a World Cup to come the following summer.

The assistant coach Bev read out the team sheet at breakfast that day. Keira was named in midfield to win her sixth cap, while Leah was among the substitutes. It would have been natural for Leah to feel envious, but her emotions were the exact opposite. Instead, Leah would be Keira's biggest fangirl, thrilled her best friend would wear the Number 4 shirt. They had already shared so much together on their footballing journeys so far: their time as young Lionesses, spells on the sidelines with similar ankle injuries. They'd even got their first senior call-up on the same day. Some things were just meant to be.

The kick-off in Moscow quickly came around and England soon forgot they were playing on a plastic pitch. They were 2–0 up within half an hour, with goals scored by Nikita Parris and Jill Scott. Russia struck back next to threaten England's lead, but Jill headed home her second goal before half-time. The second half saw Russia drop deeper, barely venturing out of their own half. All three points would surely be England's.

Then with ten minutes to go, Leah got the nod.

Deep breaths, thought Leah, slowing her breathing as the nerves bubbled up inside her.

'You'll be going on for Keira when you've warmed up,' said Bev.

Please no! thought Leah. *Anyone but Keira!* She knew her best friend would be fuming at being subbed. So, as Leah stood on the sidelines ready to go on, she practised her sternest game-face.

But Leah need not have worried. When Keira spotted the electronic board showing Leah's Number 14 to come on, she dashed straight over, an enormous grin spread across her face.

'If it were anyone else,' joked Keira, as the pair exchanged a quick hug.

'Get off!' laughed Leah, suddenly feeling emotional.

Finally, Leah had made it to the pitch, and she took

her place in midfield. England clung on for ten more minutes until the final whistle sounded.

'The first of many,' said match captain Lucy Bronze, congratulating her at the end of the match.

Leah's debut had been short and sweet, but representing her country wearing the Lionesses shirt, Leah had never felt prouder. She wished she could do it all over again.

2019: WOMEN'S WORLD CUP

On 8 May 2019, twenty-three Lionesses learned they had made the final cut for England's World Cup squad that summer. The strong competition for places gave manager Phil Neville a serious selection headache, and delivering the news to the players that had missed out had been horrible. The injured Jordan Nobbs and Izzy Christiansen, two important players for England, were among those sadly not on the plane to France.

The squad definitely had the potential to go deep into the tournament, with more English players featuring in the world's top fifty than ever before.

Neville scoured the English Women's Super League as well as the top leagues in France, Germany, Spain and USA, where some talented Lionesses played their club football, to find his favoured twenty-three.

Experience of playing in big games would be vital if England were to succeed. Karen Carney and Jill Scott would play in the World Cup for an incredible fourth time, while striker **Ellen White** hoped her third time would prove to be lucky. Captain Steph Houghton, like Karen and Jill, had over a hundred caps for England and would lead from the heart of the team's defence.

Right-back **Lucy Bronze** had emerged to become one of the best players in the world, after shooting to fame four years earlier at the World Cup in Canada. There, England had flown under the radar, winning bronze medals and returning as heroes to the flag-waving crowds that had assembled at Heathrow.

Joining those stars were the bright young talents of **Beth Mead**, Georgia Stanway, Keira Walsh and **Leah Williamson**, all thrilled to be given the chance to play against the world's best at their first major tournaments.

Completing the squad were defenders Millie Bright, Rachel Daly, Alex Greenwood, Abbie McManus and Demi Stokes, midfielders Jade Moore and Lucy Staniforth and forwards Toni Duggan, Fran Kirby, Nikita Parris and Jodie Taylor.

Now the preparation could begin. In a few short weeks, the Lionesses would be ready to take on the world in France in a tournament that was set to be *fantastique*!

CHAPTER 13

LUCY BRONZE
BIG-STAGE BRONZE

Dropping a player with such talent and even more potential never crossed the minds of the coaches that came in after Hope Powell. In 2015 World Cup qualifying, Lucy and her new Manchester City teammate Steph Houghton became the number one pairing in central defence for England too. But in early 2015, injury struck again and Lucy needed more surgery on her knee. She faced a race against time to be fit for the World Cup.

A few months later, Lucy breathed a sigh of relief when the squad for Canada was announced. But after losing their opening match to France, coach Mark Sampson decided his England team needed a shake-up. For the match that followed, Lucy was moved from left- to right-back, taking the spot of her good friend Alex Scott.

Since Lucy had joined the Lionesses, she and Alex had made a great connection. Both fierce competitors, the pair shared the same mentality: to be the best. They pushed each other all the way, but it was always healthy competition.

'You've got this, Lucia!' Alex smiled, feeling like a proud big sister.

'You don't mind I'm playing?' gasped Lucy.

'I'm just glad we have another top right-back!' Alex laughed.

The same as for Lucy, side came before self, every time. *If someone is better than me, fitter, stronger, then they should be the one to wear the shirt*, thought Alex.

Two wins followed England's opening defeat and they advanced from their group to set up a tie with Norway. Never before had they won in the knockout rounds of a World Cup. It was all to play for.

Lucy was starting as the team's right-back, with

Alex on the subs' bench. Warming up, Lucy was focused. She'd be ready for whatever the Norwegians tried to throw at her, even if it was the kitchen sink! This could be history in the making.

'Look out for their counter attacks,' Alex shouted over the noise from the crowd before kick-off. 'But remember, Luce, if you're up the field and the ball drops to you, don't be afraid to shoot.'

So in the seventy-sixth minute, with the scores tied at 1–1, that's exactly what Lucy did. Finding herself in space, twenty-five yards out from goal, Lucy knew this was her moment.

'*SHHOOOOOTTTTT!*' cried Alex, jumping to her feet from the bench.

As soon as the ball left her foot, Lucy knew it was a goal. The Norwegian goalkeeper got a hand to it, but Lucy's rocket shot had so much power that all the keeper could do was to push it into the roof of the net. It was a goal that fans would talk about for years to come!

England were riding the crest of a wave when they faced their next opponents, but hosts Canada were among the favourite teams to win the tournament.

Over 54,000 expectant fans filled the stadium in Vancouver, confident of a Canadian win.

So, when England scored twice early on, the hosts were left with a lot of work to do. Jodie Taylor scored a glorious goal before Lucy doubled the lead. When she somehow found herself on the end of a Fara Williams free kick into the box, a looping header over the goalkeeper saw the right-back score her second tournament goal.

'Told ya so!' Alex hugged Lucy at the final whistle.

The Lionesses' fairy tale sadly ended in the semi-finals, when a late own goal saw Japan sneak through, but England bounced back to beat European Champions Germany in a match that decided the bronze medal. It had taken a penalty in extra time, but England had won!

Flying home with their first ever World Cup medals, England were history-makers! Lucy was selected in the team of the tournament and named England's player of the year. A fantastic World Cup, the Lionesses had done the nation proud.

*

'You're the best player in the world,' the next England coach Phil Neville told Lucy.

Lucy shrugged off the compliment, but Phil certainly wasn't the only person in football to think so. By the summer of 2019, Lucy was at the very top of her game. She'd reached heights in football that only a handful of players ever get to experience. She had seamlessly fitted in at Lyon, the best club in Europe, where she had just won her second Champions League medal. Now the World Cup was in France too, and Lucy was raring to go with England.

The Lionesses emerged from the group stage with maximum points, before battling through a heated match with Cameroon in the Round of 16. Lucy had played every minute so far, catching the eye with her driving runs, but she knew from experience that tougher tests lay ahead.

'My bread and butter is the big games where I can make a difference,' Lucy told a packed press conference on the eve of the quarter-final.

By now, Lucy had become a pro at interviews. She even spoke to the press in French at her club, Lyon. She thought about how far she had come since her schooldays, where nearly all her conversations took place on a football pitch.

'You scored a worldie against Norway two years ago,' one reporter asked. 'Can we expect another Lucy Bronze special tomorrow night?'

Lucy laughed. 'My first job is as a defender,' she smiled. 'But if I can help the team by scoring a goal, I'll certainly try my best.'

Journalists loved her modesty and so did the fans.

And as luck would have it, Lucy did score against Norway. Her sensational volley was the cherry on the cake at the Stade Océane to make it 3–0! It was a strike that was voted the goal of the championship, while Lucy again made team of the tournament, claiming the Silver Ball behind Megan Rapinoe.

Sadly, in the semi-finals, England's opponents USA were just too strong. While Alex Morgan scored for the Americans, England missed a penalty for their chance to go level, and the match slipped away from

England. At the whistle, Lucy lay poleaxed on the grass for she didn't know how long. Nothing anyone could say could make her feel better. Not Demi, not Keira, not anyone.

'It wasn't supposed to happen this way!' she cried, unable to stop the tears.

But the USA had ripped up the script.

CHAPTER 14

LEAH WILLIAMSON TAKING ON THE WORLD

Leah was at a shopping centre in London the day the World Cup squad was announced. Shopping was something she loved to do on her rest days. Her fashion sense had come a long way since the days of only wearing football kits, now she styled designer bits with her best high-street buys.

BZZZZZ! Leah felt in her pocket for her phone. Keira's name flashed up on the screen.

'Have you read your email??!!' Keira screamed down the line.

Leah put Keira on speaker, as her phone began to buzz and ping uncontrollably.

'WE'RE GOING TO FRANCE!' Keira shrieked.

The emotions hit Leah all at once. Shock, joy, but most of all pride. She'd longed with every cell in her body to be in that squad, but to actually hear the words...

'What have we done here?' Leah gasped as the tears came fast.

'There's a video too,' Keira told her friend. 'Check it out!'

Normally the Football Association just sent out a squad list, but this time they had taken the unusual step of revealing the squad on social media. A different celebrity had recorded a special video to announce each player.

The first place confirmed was skipper Steph Houghton, with Prince William describing her as a 'defensive rock'.

Wow! thought Leah. Steph deserves that! Leah watched on smiling, as more teammates were revealed, by stars such as Emma Watson and David Beckham. Retired footballer Ian Wright appeared next.

'Somebody that I've got a lot admiration for, fantastic player...' Wrighty began, and continued:

'Lifelong Arsenal supporter, Leah Williamson!'

Leah couldn't help it, she was gone! Shoppers raised eyebrows and gave disapproving glances as they passed her, but Leah didn't notice a single one.

Only a couple of months earlier, Leah had been chosen for the SheBelieves Cup squad, a tournament hosted by the world's number one side, United States. Playing in the packed, noisy stadiums had made the hairs on her arms stand on end. It was just how she imagined the atmosphere at a World Cup to be.

England had come home on a high. They had won the trophy for the first time, and were unbeaten in all three matches against massive teams, beating Brazil and Japan and drawing with the hosts USA. To go to the States and win had felt amazing, and Leah was glad to have played her part on the pitch. But Leah, like all the players, knew their victory was just a stepping stone. If they didn't perform at the World Cup, all their hard work would count for nothing.

*

5 June 2019, Nice, France

The squad checked into their team hotel on Nice's Promenade des Anglais to be greeted by a choir of schoolchildren. Their rendition of 'Three Lions' had been so sweet – the perfect welcome to France! It wasn't that long ago since Leah had been their age, herself standing in awe before famous football players. The sunny *Côte d'Azur* would be England's base for the next few weeks, and the ideal place to relax whenever the girls had some downtime.

As the tournament kicked off, the pressure was on holders USA and hosts France as favourites. The group games quickly came and went, with Leah an unused sub. The fact that England took maximum points in their games against Scotland, Argentina and Japan made warming the bench easier for Leah to swallow. And it was such a strong, talented team!

'When the call comes, I need to be ready,' she said patiently.

In the next round, England were drawn against Cameroon in Valenciennes. By the end of the first hour, England were 3–0 up, but that score line only told half the story. The first goal came when the ref awarded England a free kick, following a Cameroon back-pass to the keeper. Steph drilled the ball through a crowded goalmouth to score, riling the Cameroon players. Next Lucy flicked the ball through to Ellen. Completely unmarked in the box, Ellen easily tucked her shot home. The ref blew for offside, but the VAR team changed her mind. England had scored fair and square, but their opponents didn't agree. When Cameroon scored next, this time the goal was judged offside. The match was threatening to boil over!

England added their third, an Alex Greenwood finish from a corner, before Cameroon escaped a penalty and a red card. Cool heads for the final minutes would be needed. When the manager gestured for to Leah to come on, she didn't flicker. She had worked her whole life for this moment.

Knowing her whole family were watching from the stands as the crowd applauded her onto the pitch meant so much. Leah thought of all the little girls and boys watching back home on TV too. It was magical.

At last, after seven long minutes of added time, the ref blew her whistle.

The game had been scrappy and ugly, not exactly how Leah had imagined her World Cup debut would play out. Still, she had made her first tournament appearance, one she wasn't likely to forget! It didn't matter in the end. The team had stayed calm throughout, and showed an incredible team spirit. England were through!

CHAPTER 15

BETH MEAD
FIRST ELEVEN

As the summer of 2019 approached, Beth was playing better than ever for her club.

'I'm not here to make up the numbers,' she told herself. 'I've got to perform week-in, week-out.'

Every day, whether it was on the pitch or in the gym, she was one hundred per cent focused. Two seasons ago she had been dropped, and not one time since had she taken her place in the starting line-up for granted. Which meant she had to stay fit.

In the club gym that day, Beth was lifting weights. Ten lifts of the heavy kettlebell with her right arm, then ten with her left. As she continued her workout, her thoughts began to drift. Always in her head was an even bigger goal. A place in England's World Cup squad would mean the absolute world to her. She had dreamed about lifting the World Cup trophy at least a million times.

So when Arsenal legend Kelly Smith announced in a video message that the young winger was going to France, Beth could barely string a sentence together!

'Not like you to be speechless, Meado!' laughed her Gunners' teammate, Jordan Nobbs, from the mat next to Beth's.

'Just wish you were coming too, Jords,' Beth said sincerely.

Jordan Nobbs was one of England's most creative midfielders. The team's vice-captain, she had won over fifty caps for the Lionesses. The two had known each other since they were kids, and had met for the first time at Middlesbrough's academy. When Beth had joined Arsenal, they had become housemates as well as teammates. Beth used to joke that she was Jordan's biggest fangirl.

Sadly though, Jordan's hopes of playing in France had been ended by a dreaded ACL injury, five months earlier. She was only halfway through her rehab and her absence would be a big disappointment for England.

Staying free of injury was a worry for any footballer. One bad tackle or an awkward landing could see a player sidelined for months. Beth had already learned that the hard way.

'You can't get rid of me that easily,' Jordan smiled kindly. 'I'll be there as England's number one fan!'

*

Seeing her name in the first eleven for England's opening match was a dream come true for Beth. She was starting on the left wing, against home nations rivals Scotland. What a match!

What made it extra special was that her family were going to be watching from the stands in the sun-drenched Stade de Nice.

It was a fixture that England couldn't take lightly. The Scotland team was made up of many players from the Women's Super League and it was bound to be a fiery encounter.

Goals from Nikita Parris and Jodie Taylor put England 2–0 by half-time, but in the second half the Lionesses seemed to take their foot off the gas. After ninety minutes, it was 2–1. It hadn't been pretty – but it was the right result.

'Three points are what counts in tournaments,' captain Steph Houghton told her team in the post-match huddle. 'We can build on this.'

After the match, Beth dashed to find her family in the far stand. Her mum and dad gave her a huge hug and told her just how proud they were.

'I'll make you even prouder,' Beth replied. 'Watch this space.'

Next up were Argentina, the weakest team in the group. England were expected to easily beat them. This time Beth grabbed her first assist, crossing to the far post for Jodie to tap in. Three more points for England. Job done.

It wasn't until the quarter-finals that Beth got her second assist. Hands on hips, she stood over the ball to take the free kick. Everyone expected her to put a cross into the box, but Beth spotted a teammate in acres of space. She pulled back the ball to Lucy, who smashed her shot into the roof of the net. Unstoppable! Norway were beaten, but a stronger opponent would try to tame the Lionesses next.

The United States. Three-time winners and the reigning champions.

It's in the bag, Beth tried to convince herself, but her heart racing in her chest told a different story.

She looked around the stadium in Lyon where over 50,000 fans were clapping and cheering feverishly. The St George flags. The home-made banners. The face-painted girls and boys, dancing in their seats.

This is what it's all about, she thought.

In a tense first half, it was the USA who broke the deadlock with a Christen Press header. Just minutes later, Beth delivered a dangerous ball to Ellen White on the edge of the six-yard box. Ellen was on the best form of her life, and expertly finished the chance.

As well as cheers for Ellen, Beth heard her own name ringing around the ground.

'Meado! Meado!' the England fans chanted.

Then right before the hour mark, Beth's number was up. Fran Kirby replaced her, as England tried to get back in the game. Sadly, it wasn't to be for England, and the USA went on to win.

In her first major tournament, Beth had played every match with her heart on her sleeve. The team had given everything. The performances of Beth and her fellow Lionesses had won many new fans in France, while attracting record TV audiences back home. Almost twelve million viewers had watched England go head-to-head with the USA. Incredible!

After the tournament, the Lionesses had some holiday. Beth headed home to Hinderwell for some time out with the family. She sat at the kitchen table reading the newspaper clippings her family had been saving. England had won so many new fans! Beth felt so proud of the Lionesses' achievements, but there was more to come. She just knew it.

CHAPTER 16

ELLEN WHITE
WORLD CUP WOE

The last time they had played in a World Cup, England had come home with an unexpected bronze medal in a tournament they would never forget. Just minutes away from a first World Cup final in Canada, their hopes were ended by an injury-time own goal. Still, collecting her bronze medal ranked as Ellen's proudest moment in an England shirt so far.

Then, on her return from another bad knee injury, Ellen had mostly played the role of super sub, and hadn't managed to get on the scoresheet. Zero goals was a stat that the striker was keen not to repeat in France.

Four years on, the mood in the camp was positive

and so was Ellen's. With twenty-eight England goals, she was now the first-choice striker but she knew that she had to keep scoring to keep her place. Three goals in the group stage matches settled the nerves.

'You're on fire, Ells!' skipper Steph Houghton congratulated her after the Japan game.

Next, came the knockout rounds. Wins against Cameroon and Norway followed with England never looking likely to exit the competition early. Ellen bagged first-half strikes in each match, taking her tally to five goals altogether. Everything she touched seemed to turn to gold!

'ELLEN WHITE-WHITE-WHITE!' sang the English supporters in the stands.

England had made the final four for the second World Cup in a row and were heading to Lyon full of confidence.

Their next opponents though were three-time world champions the United States. A squad packed with talent, their winning mentality was legendary. When the match at the Parc Olympique Lyonnais kicked off, England were very much billed as the underdogs.

True to form, the USA scored first, with winger Christen Press heading home in the tenth minute. Keeper Carly Telford had no chance of stopping that one.

Minutes later, Keira fired an incredible diagonal ball out to Beth on the left wing. This was the moment. Beth coolly delivered a pinpoint pass towards Ellen's outstretched boot. The connection was perfect – Ellen's sensational volley found the top corner to level the scores. *GOOOOAAALLL!*

Game on! There was just time for one of Ellen's famous 'goggles' celebrations, and then it was back to work. England would have to produce something special if they were to take the lead. Instead, it was the USA who quickly went back in front. Alex Morgan took advantage of a free header, as England's defence was caught napping. The American striker's goal celebration, pretending to sip a cup of tea, was deliberately designed to wind up her English opponents.

'Come on, England! We've got to do better,' Ellen roared to her teammates.

At half-time, it was 2–1, with everything still to play for.

'Just one chance. It's all I need,' Ellen promised her teammates in the dressing room.

It wasn't until the sixty-seventh minute that a clear chance to score presented itself. Keira flashed a pass to Jill, who flicked the ball on to Ellen. She scampered into the box, releasing a cool strike to the keeper's right and into the back of the net.

The 'goggles' came out once more, but England's celebrations were cut short when the referee signalled that the Video Assistant Referee was taking a look at the goal.

'Ref! There was *no way* that was offside!' Ellen argued.

'VAR will decide,' the stony-faced ref replied.

The goal was disallowed.

Pressure. It was part and parcel of the game. In the biggest match of her life, Ellen couldn't let it get to her now.

'Let's stay calm.' Steph gestured to her teammates, pushing both hands flat towards the pitch.

The next flashpoint happened in the seventy-ninth minute. As Demi Stokes slid a pass from the left towards the penalty spot, Ellen drew back her leg to shoot, but instead she missed and tumbled to the floor. Had the USA defender caught Ellen's trailing leg? The Brazilian ref hadn't thought so, but the VAR team disagreed. After a long break in play, England had a penalty! If they scored this, the Lionesses were back in with a chance of making the final.

Up stepped the Lionesses captain to take the penalty kick.

'Come on, Steph!' Ellen whispered through gritted teeth.

But as soon as it left the skipper's boot, Ellen could tell it wasn't going in. Steph's tame shot was smothered by the goalkeeper, who guessed the right way. The crowd gasped all at once, the England fans in disbelief and USA fans in sheer relief.

Ellen turned her back to goal as the USA players formed a huge red swarm around their keeper Alyssa Naeher. She couldn't bear it.

'We've got your back, Steph,' Ellen tried to console

her friend. 'Just taking that penalty shows how brave you are.'

Minutes later, things went from bad to worse, as defender Millie Bright was shown a second yellow card for a clumsy challenge. England's last throw of the dice would have to come from one of the ten players left on the pitch. But try as they might, they just couldn't hold onto the ball, while the USA attackers pushed deep into the corners.

Then, *PEEEEEEEPPPP!*

That was it. Game over. The holders had reached their third World Cup final in a row while England's luck had run out.

It was a heartbreaking way for England to bow out of the tournament. Once again, they had been a whisker away from reaching the final for the first time in their history.

Ellen turned and clapped the 53,000 supporters in the crowd. As she thought about everything that she and her teammates had achieved in France, a wave of emotion suddenly washed over her. Tears began to stream down her face, like a tap that couldn't be turned off.

England couldn't let their hard work count for nothing, they just couldn't. This squad would carry the heartache into their next tournament, determined not to be on the losing side again.

While the Lionesses' World Cup in France hadn't ended with a medal, Ellen had played out of her skin. Her six goals had seen her finish the competition as the joint top scorer, winning her the Bronze Boot. And she'd been just millimetres from turning the colour of her trophy to gold. Agony!

The next big tournament would be the European Championship, played in England. Would Ellen get the chance to shine on home soil? She had never felt hungrier for success.

2022: WOMEN'S EURO

Thursday, 16th June 2022

The day had finally arrived. The day of the squad announcement for the 2022 Women's Euro. Which twenty-three talented players were in, and who would sadly miss out? It was an anxious wait for the Lionesses to learn their fate, while millions more fans also waited desperately for the big reveal.

The tournament was kicking off a whole year later than planned, as the men's Euros had been delayed following the COVID-19 pandemic. Wembley Stadium couldn't host two finals! But now their time had come, it was time for the women to entertain the nation.

Gareth Southgate's side had brought so much joy to England fans in the summer of 2021, only for their Euro dream to end in a painful penalty shoot-out. Could the Lionesses go one step further and bring the trophy home, in their first final since 1984? Not one player from Sarina Wiegman's squad was even born back then! If they did reach Wembley, the Lionesses knew that anything could happen.

Their group games would be played in three

different stadiums, giving fans up and down the country the chance to see the host nation in action, with the opener to be played at a sold-out Old Trafford.

Experience would be priceless in such massive games. Players needed to be able to soak up the pressure and handle the expectations of the crowd. So, it came as no surprise when right-back **Lucy Bronze** was named among seven defenders.

The Lionesses' record goalscorer **Ellen White** would wear the Number 9 shirt again and be a vice-captain too. **Beth Mead**, able to conjure goals for teammates and score herself, would join England's forward line.

And **Leah Williamson** would lead the Lionesses as captain at her first European Championship, after time had run out for Steph Houghton to recover from injury.

The squad had grown and evolved in the three years that had passed since the World Cup in France. Nine new faces were taking part in their first big tournament, fearless young Lionesses hungry for success. Included were:

Young goalkeepers, Ellie Roebuck and

Hannah Hampton;

The defensive duo of Jess Carter and Lotte Wubben-Moy;

Meanwhile, Alessia Russo, Ella Toone, Lauren Hemp, Chloe Kelly and Bethany England were all set to bring firepower to England's attack.

Not forgetting the new boss, Sarina Wiegman. A woman who had led her home nation the Netherlands to glory in the previous Euros. She knew how to take a talented squad and mould them into winners, but could she do it again? England were unbeaten since Sarina had taken charge, but was it even possible for a coach to win the trophy with two different countries? Europe was about to find out.

CHAPTER 17

BETH MEAD
THE ROAD TO GOLD

6 July 2022, Old Trafford, Manchester
Women's Euro 2022 Group A match – England vs
Austria

Beth almost had to pinch herself to remind her that she was really here. An England regular, the winger had been dramatically left out of the Team GB squad that had competed at the Olympic Games the previous summer. While the rest of the Lionesses travelled to Tokyo, Beth was left at home, devastated.

The rejection had hit her hard. A mixture of anger, frustration and feelings of 'I'm not good enough' set in. But those around her knew what Beth could offer.

Her stats, eleven goals and eight assists for Arsenal that season, spoke for themselves.

'Keep going and enjoy your football,' former Lioness Kelly Smith had told her.

So that's just what Beth did. On the training pitch and in the gym, Beth worked her socks off, ready for the season ahead.

Then with Sarina Wiegman as England's new head coach, everything changed. Beth turned herself into a goal-scoring machine! Fourteen goals and ten assists in fifteen games since Sarina had taken charge had seen Beth transformed into one of England's most important players. It was exactly the fresh start that she had needed.

'You can't not pick Meado!' a Lionesses fan said, flicking through the matchday programme.

'The squad's so strong though,' said another. 'Toone and Kelly both deserve a game.'

But despite the other fantastic options in attack, Sarina put her faith in Beth.

Now the Arsenal player found herself standing in the tunnel at a packed Old Trafford as one of the chosen eleven. Almost 69,000 fans had come to see England begin their Euros adventure, the biggest ever crowd in the competition's history. Fireworks exploded and rain lashed down. The atmosphere was electric!

As the teams ran onto the pitch, the England fans burst into song:

> *'Beth Mead's on Fire,*
> *Your defence is terrified...'*

Beth clapped her hands above her head in appreciation. If England were to go far in the tournament, the fans would have such an important role to play. She looked down at the Three Lions on the England badge shining back at her.

Any player who wears this shirt has to perform, Beth thought to herself. If not, there were plenty of young Lionesses on the bench eager for minutes.

Amid deafening cheers, England made a nervy start. They would have to show they could handle the pressure. Then an early chance came. Lauren

Hemp passed to Fran Kirby, who delivered a beautiful ball into the box. Beth timed her run perfectly, beating the offside trap. Cool as ice, she chested it down and dinked the ball over Austrian keeper Manuela Zinsberger. Was it over the line? Yessss! GOOOOAAAALLLLL!!!!! England were off the mark!

Beth went straight to the fans to celebrate as they happily sang her name again. Relieved hugs from teammates Georgia Stanway and Ellen White followed, the first players to reach Beth in the box.

'Get in, Beth!' buzzed Georgia.

'Where did you learn to do that?' Ellen added.

After that, England's players settled down and the game began to flow. Beth's goal had given the whole team confidence. They would do everything to defend their lead.

In the second half, it was time for fresh legs. On went Ella Toone, Alessia Russo and Chloe Kelly for Fran, Ellen and Beth in a triple substitution. There was no disappointment from the players going off; they trusted the manager as much as she trusted them. Sarina's expert tactics would get them through the competition.

Beth left the field to a standing ovation, and was greeted by a beaming Sarina on the sidelines.

Watching the rest of the match from the bench, Beth looked out at her teammates on the pitch. Such talented players. Strong. Determined. Lionesses! Just the sort of role models she would have loved as a little girl. She felt so lucky to be in this squad.

My first goal and our first win. Beth was satisfied with how the match had gone. Her solo effort had been enough to earn all three points. It was just one match, she knew, and much tougher tests stood between England and the trophy, yet somehow it seemed bigger. It felt like a tiny jigsaw-piece of history, the start of something special.

With Manchester done, England would next travel to Brighton on the south coast. If they won there, they would be through to the next round with a game to spare. But Norway were a dangerous side with some brilliant players. To advance they would have to find a way to stop Ada Hegerberg, the all-time top scorer of the Champions League.

CHAPTER 18

ELLEN WHITE
WHITE ON THE DOUBLE

11 July 2022, Falmer Stadium, Brighton
Women's Euro 2022 Group A match – England vs
Norway

After claiming all three points in Manchester, the
fans were in a confident mood as they spilled into
Brighton's sunny stadium. While the Austria match
hadn't been a classic, the team had shown they were
united, talented and willing to work hard. Could this
be the squad to end all those years of hurt? The fans
couldn't help but start to dream.

What happened next was incredible. And no one
saw it coming. Not the players. Not the press. Not

even the fans. The Lionesses' demolition of Norway was a match that would go down in history.

Sarina had stuck with the same eleven to start against Norway. Lucy Bronze, Rachel Daly, Millie Bright – these were all players with big-game experience. Ellen White took up her Number 9 role once more too.

Ellen had played well against Austria, holding the ball up and creating space for her teammates. The only thing missing for her in that game had been a goal. In total, she was up to fifty England goals now, and was the team's record goalscorer. If she scored another three, she would be on equal goals with the Three Lions' top scorer, Wayne Rooney.

'It would be a nice milestone to reach,' Ellen told the press. 'But it really doesn't matter who scores for the team.' It was a question she had been expecting!

It was clear to all that Ellen meant every word. Now thirty-three years old, this might be her last tournament for her country. Twelve years had gone by since she pulled on her first Lionesses shirt, years that had felt like a whirlwind. She would give every last drop of energy for this team.

Her first contribution was to win a penalty, going down in the box after a tap from Norway defender Maria Thorisdottir. Foul! Ellen handed the ball to Georgia Stanway, who smashed England's opening goal home in the twelfth minute. That was the thing Ellen loved most about this younger generation – they were absolutely fearless!

Another young Lioness scored next, when Lauren flicked in a pass from Beth. VAR took a look, but ruled the goal onside. The England fans were on their feet!

Next it was Ellen's turn to get on the scoresheet. With Thorisdottir snapping at her heels, Ellen easily shrugged off the tackle. She burst into the box and unleashed a smart shot into the back of the net. As she sprinted to celebrate with the crowd, a surge of adrenaline rushed through her body.

'The Lionesses are running away with it!' the TV commentator said gleefully.

Two more quick goals from Beth came next that left the match commentators struggling to speak. Ellen glanced at the scoreboard quickly to check she wasn't dreaming. It read 5–0, and there were still seven minutes to go until half-time!

And before the ref could blow her whistle, Ellen had added a sixth, getting on the end of a cross at the far post from Fran Kirby. Sensational!

After fifty-seven minutes, Sarina decided on another triple substitution. Ellen went off to a hero's reception, having barely stopped running the whole match.

A first tournament goal for Alessia Russo and Beth's third, to claim her hat-trick, saw the match end: England 8 Norway 0. Norway had been well and truly demolished! Their star Ada Hegerberg had barely had a kick!

With the biggest score ever in a Women's Euros match, the Lionesses were creating history at every turn. What's more, they had made it look like a kickabout in the park.

More goals followed against Northern Ireland, England's last match of the group stage. A final score of 5–0 to the Lionesses meant they sailed through to the knockouts having easily scored more goals than any other team.

*

Back at the team hotel the next day, it was time to relax and take stock. The chilly ice baths were an ideal way to help tired muscles recover faster, but not every player was keen!

'I'll never get used to these!' said Jill, inching slowly into the water.

Ella Toone and Alessia giggled.

Ellen had just finished her session and was huddled up in a robe close by. She enjoyed the downtime when the squad could come together and just chat. It didn't matter how many caps you had or which club team you played for, Sarina had created an environment where everyone was equal. It also gave players like Ellen, Lucy and Jill the chance to pass on their experience of playing in the biggest matches at World Cups and Euros to the younger players.

In the tournament so far England had played well, but really they were only just getting started. A host of strong teams were still in the competition. France. Netherlands. Germany. All three had looked menacing in the group stage, and all three had knocked England out of major competitions during Ellen's time as a Lioness.

'We've got to keep pushing,' Ellen tried to explain. 'One slip-up and we could be out.'

Jill shared a story about how the players had stayed up all night following the Lionesses' defeat to USA at the World Cup. 'I wouldn't wish that heartache on anyone,' she said, suddenly serious.

In a couple more days England would travel back to Brighton for their quarter-final tie where Spain would be their opponents. *La Roja* had been tipped by many to win the tournament, but they had looked far from their best so far.

'Putellas and Hermoso may be out injured,' said Ellen. 'But they've still got quality players.'

Ellen's message was loud and clear. The Lionesses had to be ready.

CHAPTER 19

LUCY BRONZE GOLDEN BRONZE

Like Jill, Lucy was left devastated by England's semi-final defeat at the World Cup. With the tournament in her adopted country and on the best form of her life, Lucy had one hundred per cent believed England would win. When that didn't happen, it took her much longer than she'd hoped to recover. But when she did, she emerged stronger. The experience had taught her a valuable lesson: that even at your best, things could still go wrong. Three years later, Lucy was more determined than ever to try to win a trophy with England.

When the Lionesses were drawn against Spain in their Euros quarter-final, Lucy was thrilled. Only weeks earlier she had signed for Spanish champions Barcelona, a club where many of Spain's superstars played.

'The coffees are on me if you help me beat my new teammates!' she joked on the way to the stadium in Brighton, knowing just how to tempt a team of coffee-lovers. She hated the stuff herself.

'Yessss!' cheered the whole bus. Not that they needed any extra motivation.

A win would not be easy though. Spain had developed into a top team these past few years. Players like Bonmatí and del Castillo could be a real handful. The away team began brightly and looked the more likely to score in the first half, but it was Ellen who found the back of the net first. Offside!

Lucy had been in an offside position when the cross came in to Ellen, but she was sure she hadn't touched the ball. 'Let's keep going!' she rallied.

Instead it was Spain's Esther González who managed to break the deadlock, stroking the ball past Mary Earps in the fifty-fourth minute. The crowd went so silent that the only English voices in the stadium came from the commentary box. Spain were on top.

England had to respond or they would be out.

On came Manchester United teammates Alessia and Ella, who reignited the fire in the Lionesses. With just six minutes to go, the pair combined perfectly. Alessia nodded the ball to Ella who volleyed home the equaliser. What a duo!

Spanish heads went down, while England kept on pushing. Then in extra time, the winning goal came. Georgia Stanway picked up the ball in midfield and drove on towards the box. With the Spain defenders backing off, Georgia picked her spot and smashed the ball past Sandra Paños. *Gooooooaaaaallll!*

It was a strike that almost blew the roof off the stadium, as choruses of 'It's Coming Home' rang out around the ground for the first time that night.

'We can do this!' said Lucy, as wave after wave of Spanish attacks kept coming.

The defenders used every trick in the book to keep possession, as the clock ticked down. Then, finally, they had done it. England were in the semi-finals!

Sarina led the celebrations with a fist-pump to the TV cameras, as the relieved hugs and dancing followed. The Lionesses were in a party mood and were taking the whole country along for the ride!

*

England's win against Spain had everyone believing that the trophy was in the Lionesses' hands. The fans, the press and the players too. It didn't matter whether England led or came from behind in the games, this special squad had what it took to get the right result.

Sarina had named the same starting eleven in every match so far, and incredibly, the subs she brought on were just as strong! England headed to their semi-final in Sheffield in confident mood.

It was another full house as England took on Sweden. Could the Olympic silver medallists be the team to spoil the party? As Europe's highest-ranked team, they certainly had the players.

Lucy was desperate to help her team get to Wembley. She'd played three major semi-finals with England and all three had ended in defeat. If she used the width of the pitch to create space, she knew she had a chance of making an assist. Walking out at Bramall Lane, she felt focused. Relaxed, even.

The match began at a furious pace, with Sweden piling on the pressure. The ninth minute saw the team in yellow hit the bar, but England's defence stood firm. England had to stay patient and wait for their chance to come. Then when Lauren Hemp won a corner, Beth swung in a cross to Lucy who headed narrowly wide. Close!

A little later, it was time for Lucy to return the favour. She collected the ball on the right wing and crossed to Beth who unleashed an unstoppable finish. It was goal number six of the tournament for Beth and another assist for Lucy!

Lucy had some advice for her teammate at half-time. 'If we get another corner, try to find me in the box,' she said to Beth. 'I can get a goal, I can just feel it.'

The teams returned after the break knowing the next goal would be all-important. Could Sweden fight back, or would England go further ahead? It was England! When they won a corner just minutes into the second half, there was Lucy at the far post to head the ball down and into the net. Just as she'd promised!

'Lucy Bronze strikes gold for England!' said the commentator.

'Yesss, Bronzey!' cheered Beth.

The next goal was outrageous! Keira fed in a pass to Fran Kirby, who squared it back to Alessia. Alessia saw her shot saved, but she wasn't giving up. With her back to goal in a crowded box, the only option was to backheel the ball... straight through the keeper's legs! GOOOOAAAALLLLL! ALESSIA RUSSO!

'I can't believe you just did that!' laughed Lucy, as she joined the huddle around Alessia.

And a fourth goal was the icing on the cake! When Fran chipped Hedvig Lindahl from outside the box, England's place at Wembley was sealed.

A 4–0 scoreline. A goal, an assist and more importantly, a clean sheet, thought Lucy. It had been her strongest performance of the tournament. As she went to shake hands with the deflated Swedish players, she felt strangely calm. Was this it? Was football about to come home?

CHAPTER 20

LEAH WILLIAMSON FINAL SCORE

31 July 2022, Wembley Stadium, London
Women's Euro 2022 final – England vs Germany

As the national anthems played, Leah couldn't help but smile. Her usual game-face was now banished to the bench.

'We've got a job to do, but let's enjoy every minute of this final,' she told her teammates. She knew that an occasion like this may never come around again.

The team had worked so hard to get to Wembley, winning every match on their way. Now only Germany stood between England and the trophy.

Germany's own route to the final had seen them

knock out the Netherlands and France. They had won the competition eight times before, while England had never been champions. But with the match on home soil, and thousands more England fans than German ones, the game was too close to call.

Leah took off her tracksuit jacket to reveal the rainbow armband, the same captain's armband she had worn all tournament. It felt like a dream. She had captained the side brilliantly, winning the respect of the whole squad and the hearts of Lionesses fans up and down the country. Now she would try to lead England to victory in the Women's Euro Final.

Soon after the team photos, Germany announced a last-minute change to their line-up. Their star striker and leading scorer Alex Popp would have to sit out the game, injured. How much would her loss unsettle the team?

The change left Leah's Arsenal teammate Beth with a clear path to win the Golden Boot. Only Alessia could realistically overtake her.

Onto the pitch sped the tiny rainbow car to deliver the match ball, and a tense first half kicked off moments later. By the break most of the chances had fallen to England, the best of them to Ellen and Lucy. Germany had come close from a corner too, when Leah had cleared off the line in a goalmouth scramble. VAR checked for handball, but saw no foul.

Minutes into the second half, Germany's Lina Magull fired a warning shot, but sent the ball just wide of the post. In the dugout, Sarina acted swiftly to calm jangling England nerves. On came Ella and Alessia for Fran and Ellen. The young duo's energy and fearlessness had been so important to England over the tournament so far.

Shortly after though... INJURY! Beth came off worse from a fifty-fifty tackle. Lucy helped the physio try in a desperate attempt to get Beth back on her feet, but England's top scorer couldn't carry on. Chloe Kelly replaced her.

Then a big chance came, as Keira found Ella with a perfect pass that split Germany's defence. Ella was through on goal with just the keeper to beat. Was the super sub ready to take centre stage in front of 87,000 fans at Wembley? She was! Her beautiful scooped finish over keeper Merle Frohms's head was worthy of any cup final!

'The goalscorer for England, Number 20, ELLA TOOOOOOONE!' the stadium announcer boomed to rapturous applause.

'Let's stay composed,' Leah shouted her instructions, as soon as the celebrations had died down. There was still around half an hour to go: the game could change in an instant.

Just minutes later Germany rattled the England crossbar, before Mary Earps gathered the rebound confidently. Germany and Lina Magull were getting closer.

Then in the seventy-ninth minute, the German forward equalised. She had been threatening to score the whole game, and at last her efforts had been rewarded.

'We go again,' Leah called, clapping her hands. England had to keep their cool.

With so little to choose between the two quality sides, it wasn't surprising the match went to extra time. It couldn't possibly end in a dreaded penalty shoot-out, could it?

Nooo! Because with just ten minutes of extra time remaining, Chloe poked home from a Lauren Hemp corner. *GOOOOOAAAAAAAAAALLLLLLLLLL!* The substitute took off her shirt in sheer delight and began swinging it around her head like a lasso. The ref had no choice but to show a yellow card for the celebration, but Chloe didn't care. Eleven months out through injury, she made the Euros squad by the skin of her teeth!

England were back in the lead and were not about to give it up again.

With every move that followed, Germany just couldn't get hold of the ball. England were playing for time and Germany were frustrated. Then at last the whistle blew and...

ENGLAND WERE
EUROPEAN CHAMPIONS!!!!

Incredible scenes followed. The cheers, the hugs, the tears, but most of all the singing and the dancing.

The party would carry on for days to come!

Gold medals were presented with more prizes for the players too. Keira won Player of the Match trophy, while Beth bagged the Golden Boot and the Player of the Tournament award. Then it was time for the big one. The famous Women's Euro trophy.

As Leah was handed the trophy, the smile on her face was as wide as Wembley Way! She carried it carefully to the podium where the whole squad was gathered.

'Help a girl out here?' Leah asked Millie. 'It's pretty heavy!'

'No problem, skipper!' Millie smiled back.

So together, Leah and Millie lifted the trophy, engraved with England's name for the very first time. In that moment, with that group of players and coaches to share it with her, Leah had never felt happier. Confetti rained down and fireworks boomed. She'd won trophies before, but these celebrations were on another level.

When the TV reporters finally managed to grab Leah for an interview, she had a message for everyone watching:

'We've finally done it, we've finally brought everyone together,' the passion in her voice sounded out. 'The legacy of this team is as winners and I'm so proud to be English!'

They may have just won a final, but for the Lionesses, Leah explained, it was the start of a new journey. Now the world was listening they would use their platform to blaze a trail for women's sport and give everyone the right to play football.

But first, the celebrations. Football had come home.

Read on to meet more superstars
in Sarina Wiegman's incredible
Women's Euro 2022 squad!

MEET THE TEAM

SARINA
WIEGMAN

Position: **HEAD COACH**

1 MARY
EARPS

Position: **GOALKEEPER**
Club: **MAN UNITED**
D.O.B: **7 MAR 1993**

13 HANNAH
HAMPTON

Position: **GOALKEEPER**
Club: **ASTON VILLA**
D.O.B: **16 NOV 2000**

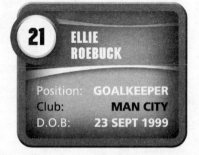

21 ELLIE
ROEBUCK

Position: **GOALKEEPER**
Club: **MAN CITY**
D.O.B: **23 SEPT 1999**

MEET THE TEAM

2 LUCY
BRONZE

Position: **RIGHT BACK**
Club: **BARCELONA**
D.O.B: **28 OCT 1991**

3 RACHEL
DALY

Position: **LEFT-BACK**
Club: **ASTON VILLA**
D.O.B: **6 DEC 1991**

5 ALEX
GREENWOOD

Position: **CENTRE/LB**
Club: **MAN CITY**
D.O.B: **7 SEPT 1993**

MEET THE TEAM

6

MILLIE BRIGHT

Position: **CENTRE-BACK**
Club: **CHELSEA**
D.O.B: **21 AUG 1993**

12

JESS CARTER

Position: **CENTRE/RB**
Club: **CHELSEA**
D.O.B: **27 OCT 1997**

8

LEAH WILLIAMSON

Position: **CENTRE-BACK**
Club: **ARSENAL**
D.O.B: **29 MAR 1997**

MEET THE TEAM

15 **DEMI STOKES**

Position: **LEFT-BACK**
Club: **MAN CITY**
D.O.B: **12 DEC 1991**

4 **KEIRA WALSH**

Position: **DEF MIDFIELD**
Club: **MAN CITY**
D.O.B: **8 APR 1997**

16 **JILL SCOTT**

Position: **CEN MIDFIELD**
Club: **UNATTACHED**
D.O.B: **2 FEB 1987**

MEET THE TEAM

22

LOTTE
WUBBEN-MOY

Position: **CENTRE-BACK**
Club: **ARSENAL**
D.O.B: **11 JAN 1999**

10

GEORGIA
STANWAY

Position: **ATT MIDFIELD**
Club: **BAYERN MUNICH**
D.O.B: **3 JAN 1999**

14

FRAN
KIRBY

Position: **ATT MIDFIELD**
Club: **CHELSEA**
D.O.B: **29 JUN 1993**

MEET THE TEAM

20

ELLA
TOONE

Position: **ATT MIDFIELD**
Club: **MAN UNITED**
D.O.B: **2 SEPT 1999**

11

LAUREN
HEMP

Position: **LEFT WING**
Club: **MAN CITY**
D.O.B: **7 AUG 2000**

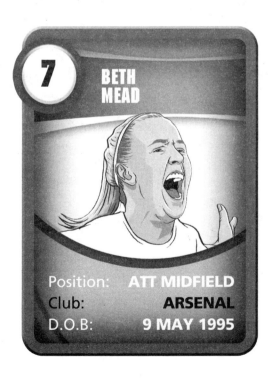

7

BETH
MEAD

Position: **ATT MIDFIELD**
Club: **ARSENAL**
D.O.B: **9 MAY 1995**

MEET THE TEAM

18

CHLOE KELLY

Position:	**RIGHT WING**
Club:	**MAN CITY**
D.O.B:	**15 JAN 1998**

9

ELLEN WHITE

Position:	**STRIKER**
Club:	**MAN CITY**
D.O.B:	**9 MAY 1989**

MEET THE TEAM

17 NIKITA PARRIS

Position:	**FORWARD**
Club:	**MAN UTD**
D.O.B:	**10 MAR 1994**

23 ALESSIA RUSSO

Position:	**FORWARD**
Club:	**MAN UNITED**
D.O.B:	**8 FEB 1999**

19 BETHANY ENGLAND

Position:	**FORWARD**
Club:	**CHELSEA**
D.O.B:	**3 JUN 1994**

Turn the page for a sneak preview of
another brilliant football story by
Charlotte Browne. . .

KIRBY

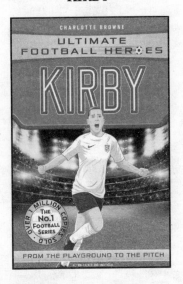

Available now!

CHAPTER 1

THE MOVE
SOUTH

'Well, it's alright,' said Stephen Kirby, sighing deeply.
'It's hardly the Pennine mountain though, is it?'

His wife Denise laughed. 'Oh Stephen, come on,
it's an area of outstanding beauty!'

'Yeah, so they might say down here, Deni, but
they haven't seen what we grew up around, have
they, eh?'

Stephen put his arm around his wife. They were
looking out across the sweeping Chiltern Hills, a short
drive, not far from their home on the outskirts of
Reading. Their two small children Frances and James
were with them.

It had been several years since the Kirbys had made

the move south from Sunderland near Tyne and Wear to Berkshire. Since then Stephen had been working night shifts with Great Western Railway, the train company. Also, Deni worked as a nurse in a nearby hospital, so this was a rare day out for them all to enjoy as a family.

'You don't regret moving, do you?' Deni asked her husband.

'What, giving up what would have been a dazzling career with Sunderland Academy?' Stephen replied with a twinkle in his eye.

Deni snorted again. 'Oh, Stephen!'

'Don't laugh! If it hadn't been for that blasted injury I'd have sent Sunderland AFC soaring up into the Premier League! Or back to our good old former glory days of '36 at least!'

She patted him on the arm. 'I'm sorry, pet, I know how much football means to you.'

'It's okay. Nah, really don't regret it. Well, you know, course I miss the River Wear. Oh, the walks along there...'

'We have the Thames!'

'Pah!'

She smiled. 'And of course, our families back home.'

'Yeah, I miss them too.' They were both silent for a moment, contemplating.

'Well, obviously I moved down here to get away from your family!'

'Oh Stephen!'

'You wouldn't get them moving down here to live with a load of southerners.'

She chuckled. 'They still look a bit puzzled when I call you "pet"!'

'I know!'

'Strange to think, our children aren't going to grow up with Geordie accents.'

'Not if I can help it!'

They looked over at their two children, Frances and James, who were playing with a football. At four and three years old respectively, barely a year between them, for the most part they played sweetly with each other. Unless a football was involved. Then gentle play often turned to outright war as they both tried to gain control of it.

'James!' Deni cried, as he tackled his younger sister to the floor. 'Careful!'

'Ah, it's in the genes,' said Stephen proudly. 'Destiny.' He actively encouraged his children's love of the sport and had taken them to a few Sunderland games already that year.

'I'll make sure I pass the mantle of greatness on to my son that's for sure,' he added.

Deni laughed. 'Oh go away with you, Stephen! Although I wouldn't underestimate your daughter's talents either!'

'No,' he said thoughtfully, 'you're right.'

They both looked on as Fran, undeterred, was back off the ground, chasing enthusiastically after her brother who was heading off down the hill. She was tiny, even for her age group, but fast on her feet and sturdy.

'Go on, Frances! Go on!' her dad encouraged. She caught her brother up, kicked the ball away from him and began to dribble it.

'See!' said Deni. 'She's quite something.'

'Natural instinct already! See – it's in the genes!'

Deni laughed. 'Well, it looks as though we might have a proper pair of football stars on our hands to coach!'

'Yeah, as long as they support Sunderland! Not Reading... heaven forbid.'

'Well at least Reading are in the First Division!'

They both laughed as they continued to stroll through the countryside and snap photos of the pair battling it out for the ball.

'We'll have to send some photos back home,' said Deni.

'*Forever my Sunderland, I will stand by you... my blood runs red and white...*'

'Oh don't sing, Stephen, it sounds bad!'

CHAPTER 2

WATCHING THIERRY

'Hai-yah – Judo chop!'

'What the?!' Stephen cried out as Fran jumped from out of a tree in their garden, landing on his back.

'Flipping 'eck!'

Deni came running out of the back door to catch sight of Fran chopping her little hand at her dad.

'Hai – ya!' she cried, thrusting her leg out towards him.

'Come on, Dad – at least *try* and block me!'

He started laughing. 'We didn't send you to judo lessons so that you could attack your own dad, you know – besides, kicks and chops are Karate, not Judo!'

She giggled. 'Resistance is futile, Dad!'

Fran was seven years old and one of the smallest in her year. Her parents had decided to send her to judo classes to ensure her height didn't affect her confidence. It appeared to be working, and she seemed happy to spar with anyone, regardless of their size.

'Okay, Dad, let's play football. I'm bored of beating you at judo.'

Deni watched as her daughter keepie-uppied with a football and began to dribble it down the garden. She marvelled at Fran's boundless energy, speed and athleticism in all her sporting activities. But it was notable that, when the girl had a ball at her feet, a huge smile spread out across her face and her big brown eyes began to twinkle.

Fran was especially fired up when she was wearing her favourite Number 14 Arsenal away strip and pretending to be her hero Thierry Henry. She recorded *Match of the Day* clips of Arsenal's new signing and endlessly replayed them, so that she could study his moves and learn all the tricks.

Still dribbling, Fran reached her dad, who was stuck in the middle of a makeshift goal cobbled together from old flowerpots.

She chattered to herself, pretending to take on opponents: 'And here he comes! He's in the middle! Cool as a cucumber! He takes on one, then another – and another! He's in the penalty box! Is he gonna shoot from there? He makes it look so easy! Get ready, Dad!'

She warned Stephen as she took aim with her left boot. 'And it is so easy! He scores!'

Her father fell to the ground as he attempted to save her shot.

'Great left boot, pet,' he said, 'but you've got to make sure your right is just as strong, we need to do some work on that.' Already, her father was one of her toughest critics.

Her mother called out: 'That's a Thierry Henry finish, Frances! Very cool!'

Her father got up, dusting himself down. He groaned. 'Ah, I dunno, why do you have to be an Arsenal fan?'

'Because I'm a Thierry Henry fan, Dad – he's amazing!'

'Now let me tell you about Sunderland's player, Mickey...'

'Oh Dad. I don't care! No-one plays like Henry on the field! I wanna play like him one day!' Already at seven, Fran could identify her idol's ability on both the wing and as a lone striker, that could easily take on players one on one.

'You will play like him!' her mum called out from the kitchen. 'Better than him! Arsenal will want you in no time!'

'Sunderland!' her dad protested.

'Mmm, Mum,' said Fran. 'Are you cooking what I think you're cooking? Smells delicious!'

'That's right, enchiladas, your favourite!'

'When I grow up, Mum, all I'm ever going to eat is enchiladas! They're the best!'

'Hmm, I don't know if you can survive on enchiladas alone!'

'I don't care, Mum – I'm going to eat so many I'll turn into an enchilada!'

'I'll have to teach you how to make them properly.'

'Or you can just make them for me forever!'

Deni laughed as Fran ran inside and threw her arms around her. She looked into her daughter's eyes that sparkled from underneath a wave of blonde hair. Deni had long given up trying to tame or comb it. There wasn't much point – she was always out playing.

Fran grabbed her favourite enchilada – avocado with Mexican bean – and began to wolf it down.

'Frances! What's the hurry?'

'James's mates are playing football down Caversham Park. I don't wanna miss them!'

James and his friends were only a year older than her, but they seemed like giants to Fran, as they were considerably taller than she was – not that she was fazed by that. She'd always wanted to play football to be cool, like them, tagging along to join in with their games in the park. But James never discouraged her. Neither did any of his friends – if they objected, they were soon silenced when they found out how nifty she was on her feet.

The doorbell rang. James stumbled down the stairs to answer, but not before grabbing an enchilada for himself.

'Alright, sis! You ready?'

'You'll look after your sister, eh?' said Deni.

'She can look after herself!'

Fran nodded at her mum proudly. James turned to his friends, friends that Fran didn't recognise, and said: 'My sister's coming too – that alright?'

She saw them both pull a bit of a face in surprise and she smiled to herself.

'Just you wait,' she thought. Fran loved it when her brother brought friends she hadn't played with before. It was a chance to show them what she could do.

As Deni watched her daughter run off she turned to her husband. 'You know – I never see her happier than when she's about to play football. She absolutely whizzed out of that door.'

'She's very athletic, loves lots of sports.'

'She is. But I never see her eyes light up more than when she's got a ball at her feet. I think football's the sport we should really encourage her in.'

'You think she could really go far?'

'I *know*, Stephen. She's got real talent. I think she

could make it.'

'I knew living south would get to you one day, love.'

'Oh, Stephen!'

CAN'T GET ENOUGH OF
ULTIMATE FOOTBALL HEROES?

**Check out heroesfootball.com
for quizzes, games, and competitions!**

**Plus join the Ultimate Football Heroes
Fan Club to score exclusive content
and be the first to hear about
new books and events.
heroesfootball.com/subscribe/**